'Terri...'
Frank Cotterell Boyc...

'Beautifully written.'
Irish Independent

'A uniquely poetic Northern voice . . . Quirky, mysterious, humorous . . . **a joy to read**.'
MG Leonard, author of *Beeetle Boy*

'**Magical, mysterious, utterly charming**.'
Book Bag

'**A beautiful piece of fiction**.'
Countryfile

'**Unforgettable**.' ★★★★★
Books for Keeps

'Funny, sad, poignant, quirky and unique.'
Katie, age 12, Lovereading4kids

'**Distinctive and authentic** from the first page.'
Irish Times

'Full of **adventure**. Has you **hooked** from the first page.'
Isaac, age 10, Lovereading4kids

'**Utterly unusual and mesmerising**.'
Abi Elphinstone, author of *Sky Song*

'**An astonishing tale, truly special!**'
Cally, age 10, Lovereading4kids

'**Hilarious, fast-moving adventure**.'
Metro

ABOUT THE AUTHOR

Fish Boy was Chloe Daykin's first novel, which she wrote while studying for her MA in Creative Writing at Newcastle University. It won a Northern Writers' Award, was nominated for the CILIP Carnegie Medal, longlisted for the UKLA Book Awards, shortlisted for the Branford Boase and garnered critical acclaim. An artist, designer, playwright and teacher, Chloe is always up for an unusual adventure and lives in Northumberland with her family. *Fire Girl, Forest Boy* is her third novel.

BY THE SAME AUTHOR

Fish Boy
The Boy Who Hit Play

FIRE GIRL, FOREST BOY

Chloe Daykin

90 YEARS OF EXCELLENCE

FABER & FABER

First published in 2019
by Faber & Faber Limited
Bloomsbury House
74–77 Great Russell Street
London, WC1B 3DA

Typeset in Baskerville by M Rules
Printed by CPI Group (UK) Ltd, Croydon CR0 4YY
All rights reserved
Text © Chloe Daykin, 2019

The right of Chloe Daykin to be identified as author of this work
has been asserted in accordance with Section 77 of the
Copyright, Designs and Patents Act 1988

A CIP record for this book is available
from the British Library

ISBN 978–0–571–34943–2

FSC
www.fsc.org
MIX
Paper from
responsible sources
FSC® C020471

2 4 6 8 10 9 7 5 3 1

This book is dedicated to anyone who needs
a little inner fire.

If you catch the light right you can get the look on someone's face. The look that comes and goes in the bazillionth of a second.

The one you had the day the letter came. The one that promised to change our lives forever. That's as much as I saw before you shut it and yourself away in the study. 'Cept you came back out.

And it never did.

Ever.

If I had a camera –

CLICK –

I could've got it.

That look.

That and the one you had yesterday.

Before *they* came.

The people I trust as much as green mambas. (No offence to the mambas.)

And you disappeared.

If I had a camera I could've shown everyone what

their faces look like at 5 a.m. this morning when they walk into my room and tell me that you've gone. That you've left me alone. Lost in the Land of the Sun.

And if I had a camera I could show you what they look like right now when I'm hanging out of a tree in the cloud forest with a sloth. And light balls are falling out of the sky.

Maya

I don't have a camera but I do have my brain.

CLICK.

And that can take pictures no one can rub out.

And no one can make it stop.

CLICK CLICK CLICK.

I'm Maya Anderson and I've taken pictures that way since forever.

My head's like an iPhone I can scroll through. I can flip it back to playgroup, or the sandwich I had on Monday, then forward to now – and all those shots that I took are there, frozen in time.

I have memories I don't know what to do with and ones I like to visit, like an album. It's handy for faces, and for moments like when you're in the middle of the jungle in the midst of an unnatural phenomenon.

Moments like now.

Maybe if I can freeze-frame fast enough I'll find out why it's happening.

Maybe if I look close enough I can find out where you are.

And maybe if I could use my eyes like projector lenses, I could show everyone all the light that's inside me that no one ever seems to notice. And I could burn so bright I'd put a hole right through the wall and toast the feet of the lantern flies lined up on the other side.

Raul

In my life I dream of what's on the other side. Over the border from the hairy eyebrow of South America. Peru.

The Sacred Valley.

Ollantaytambo.

That's where I live.

But it isn't who I am.

The land of the Incas. We're on the Urubamba River. The town with the wild dogs who chase plastic bags in packs, and the water running in channels down the streets. Our house is on the hill. We live where the water starts to run.

Ollantaytambo's like a labyrinth, a grid of cobblestone roads. Walk around and you'll see dark open doorways, chickens wandering in and out, and plants twisting their way up and over walls, pushing their way through everything.

I wasn't always a townie – we moved here two years ago. I'm still not. In my heart.

My body disagrees though. *Call that a jump?* it

says. I can't even spring a wall. I used to shimmy up banana trunks no problem. I lived with the trees. Brick and stone and roads are new to me. Still. Even after two years it still feels weird.

The day we moved here I dreamt of escaping it. Like a frog out of a wet fist.

BOING.

Now that's a jump.

The feeling still burns inside me. My legs twitch. For the past two years they've wanted to run back home to put things right. Things that went so wrong no one thinks they can.

At night, while Mami and Papi wash dishes and dance to the radio, and my little brothers go wild in the streets, I climb out of the town and sit on the mountain staring at the stars, dreaming of how to do it, how to turn the world inside out and jump in.

Sometimes you're born knowing there's a destiny inside you. Something to take you away from where you are and into something

BIGGER.

I didn't know the answer was going to fall into my lap like a hot stone spat out of a fire, bright and strong and burning a hole through everything.

Maya

Lantern flies?

Yeah, right now we're in the Amazon Basin, Peru. Not we. Used to be we.

Now I guess I mean me.

Maya Anderson. Daughter of Dr Handi Anderson. The Light Man. That's what everyone calls him.

Everyone who knows.

Which is the world. The science world anyway.

Not that they know about me. To them I'm just a shadow, sitting at the back of the lecture hall while Dad works, lighting up the faces of everyone in the room, talking physics and particles and mysteries of the universe, and I watch with my homework (undone), an apple and a camera brain.

Seeing what everyone else doesn't.

Which is a lot.

It's amazing what people don't notice.

Sometimes I flip the pictures in my head back to my cot as a baby with my mum gone. She left when

I was three. Don't ask. No one else does. Not any more. And when no one talks about her the gap she's left gets bigger.

We have one picture of her in the flat. Just one. I think she looks like me. As I get older I think it more. I think Dad thinks so too. The way he stares at me. The way he never talks about her. The way he backs off into his work if I try to ask.

When I was little Dad put up cardboard animal mobiles that hung over candle lanterns in all the rooms of our flat. When they caught the light they danced on the walls. I used to stare up at the mobile shadows dancing, wondering where she went, like someone just snuffed the light out, like a candle.

Light.

Light is Dad's thing. It's what he researches. He believes that in its centre is 'catan' – a kind of nectar for the soul, affecting moods and dreams.

People think he's stupid.

People think he's a genius.

Fifty/fifty?

I dunno.

I think he's Dad who burns fish fingers and forgets to wash gym socks. And whose research means we get to travel all over the world, poking at ideas. Soaking up stories and sunshine. Last year it was Norway, before that the Arctic. It's how I got to meet Inuits and icebergs and Vikings.

And it's how we're here in the Amazon in the cloud forest, with dragonflies as thick as your thumb and trees with teeth spikes.

And it's how there's a woman outside my door who knocks. A woman who arrived yesterday with a man with a red face and sweat patches, who I trust as much as a bag of pit vipers. No offence to the vipers who can kill you with their sixth sense. A woman who comes in and asks me to sit down. I don't.

Who tells me that Dad's gone.

POOF.

In his own batch of cloud smoke.

And gives me a note that says he isn't coming back.

Raul

Dad works as a trail leader, bird spotter, cook. Whatever gets us the work, whatever gets us the money. It didn't used to be that way. We didn't used to need money. Not much. When we lived in the rainforest we grew and found and hunted what we needed, and traded for the rest.

We weren't cut off behind bricks and streets with light switches and taps and bills. We were free. Till we weren't. Till we were sliced apart from the jungle like a blade cutting the stone out of an avocado.

POP.

And everything changed.

These days we work and buy.

Lots of people buy.

Tourists come to the village and buy the food in the restaurants, the cloth people weave, the jewellery they make. They walk the Inca trail. Camping in the mist on mountains so high you can hardly breathe, in orange pup tents like cocoons. Standing in Inti

Punku, the Sacred Valley's sun gate, at 5 a.m., walking into Machu Picchu, the city in the sky, walking into the past.

We show them the way, how to stand aside for the porters running the paths with the tents and the food on their backs, how to tape their blisters and fill their bellies with rice and hot bananas.

Sometimes I go too, if I can help out. If I keep my head down, don't get in the way and don't cost anything.

If I keep invisible.

School doesn't like it, but school can't hold everyone. Everyone needs money and some kids I know make stuff and sell it. They'd rather have the money than the facts. What's the point of learning stuff you'll never use, about places you'll never go, things you'll never see.

Money gets you places.

Money gets results.

I like walking the trails, passing through the valley of orchids and up into the ruins, the town above the clouds. I like the way the mountains open out and the condors come. Birds as big as boats that can keep six kilos of food in their throat sack.

11

I learned that from the other guides. Condors are the birds of the gods.

People come here from all over the world. Last summer a walker called Rick from Idaho gave me his watch.

We were sitting round the campfire, looking at the sky.

He told me his daughter had died. 'What's the point in time?' he said. 'It just makes us feel in control of things we have no control over at all.' He unclicked it off his wrist and we stared at the moon.

The watch has a moon on it. It moves round with the time and the days.

When I look at the watch I think about Rick and I think he's wrong.

Days help us count down to something.

Days move us forward.

With days we can make plans.

With plans we can change who we are and who we want to be.

With plans we can escape.

Maya

Dad's been weird since he got the letter. The one that made him jump and shut himself in his study. The letter he wouldn't let me look over his shoulder and see.

We promise to change your life forever, it said.

I laughed and he didn't.

I didn't get to read any more 'cos he locked the door.

He never locks it.

Then he just locked himself and his thoughts away and told me we were going to Peru.

And here we are.

Back home we live in Glasgow in a top-floor flat with candles and big windows. Dad thinks that electric lights pollute the soul. I used to think this was fun, till I got older and didn't. Till he wouldn't let me get a phone. He tapped his forehead and said, 'Fake light pollutes the soul.' And I wanted to explode him on the spot. (These days we compromise on low-energy bulbs – dingy, but they mean all the world to me.)

In Glasgow we don't have sloths or jaguars or howler monkeys or light balls that fall out of the sky.

We have Socks, who is black and white and the floppiest cat a person could know or love. He's more of a scarf than a cat and hangs round your neck whenever you need him. He doesn't pollute anyone's soul. He soothes.

At night, me and Socks sit on my bed by the window looking at the lights flicking on in other people's houses, wondering what it's like to be them, and where me and Dad are going to end up next.

I didn't know it was going to be alone. In a jungle lodge with a maze of wooden walkways that try to keep your feet in the air and out of the way of nature and fire ants, with a woman and a man (with eyes like a frog's) who turned up while we were sitting round the fire with our guide last night. Our guide took one look and vanished into the woods, like water into the earth.

I liked our guide.

Dad looked up like he wasn't surprised, and they oozed into the camp like molten metal into a mould.

They squatted next to the fire. Their faces lit in the flames.

I looked at Dad and folded my arms. He looked at the floor.

'We are Charles and Rosa,' they said.

'Where are you from?'

'Lima University,' they said. 'We research plants.'

Their fake answers were as fake as their fake smiles on their fake faces.

They asked Dad to come into the woods to collect specimens, like it was some kind of code, and went off to the lodge to change.

Dad swallowed and held me by the shoulders in the dark and said, 'You know I love you, don't you? Whatever happens.'

Actually I don't. It's pretty hard to know it when all someone does is yell or ignore you. Which is pretty much how it goes these days.

'Whatever what happens?'

Silence.

Dad went into the lodge to change too and they left. I tried to follow, but our guide jumped out of the trees like a ghost and put a hand on my shoulder and held me back. 'No,' he said. And shook his head.

Then they were too far gone to find.

I went to bed with a really weird feeling and in the middle of the night there was a gunshot.

I snapped the torch on and looked over.

Dad's bed was empty. He was gone.

In Glasgow we don't have guns either.

Or kidnappers.

Least, not on our street.

I sat on my bed till dawn, watching the rain drip through the bullet hole in the roof, but he never came back. Charles and Rosa did. Knocking on the door with an envelope of money and the note.

And now they're in my room. These people I don't even know, trying to pack up my bags and shove me out of the door, away from the lodge and down the mud-track trail to their canoe.

Dear Maya,

By the time you are reading this I will be gone.

I am waving from the empty sheets on the other side of the room!

Don't be afraid.

Research has taken me somewhere unexpected. Somewhere I never dreamed I would go.

Please go home.

It will be safer.

Rosa will take you.

Socks and Mrs Glidings* will be waiting.

I will be home soon.

And everything will be wonderful.

I promise.

Dad

xxx

* Mrs Glidings lives downstairs. We bunk up together when Dad goes on trips, me and Socks and Mrs Glidings. She cooks ace biscuits. No way I'm going there right now though.

Raul

This trail trip is different.

When I pack I slip extra stuff into my bag. Trousers, my blue T-shirt, three bags of *cancha chulpe* salt corn kernels and my Coke can of cash from under my bed.

I made a plan last week.

It started on Tuesday after school when Aiko – with the dark eyes and the cellar with the llama foetus and skulls she says are her great-great-grandparents, but that actually she stole from up in the mountains (and everybody knows it) – shoved a linen ball into my hand, looked into my eyes and said, 'You are destined for adventure.'

Aiko's dad is the village healer, the shaman. The one in the town with magic. If people are ill here, they don't go to the doctor. They go to him. I don't like Aiko, or her floor full of guinea pigs that sound like fire crackling when they eat.

'I found it in the water.' She pointed at the

channel running down the street. 'My papi says the mountains sent it.'

I backed off out of the square. Ran up through the town and sat with my back to Papi Rosales's old wooden door, petting Toffee his dog on the head. I listened to the radio from Mami Leona's as she fried bananas, and unwound that parcel.

When I saw what was at the centre of it I knew it was a sign.

A necklace I hadn't seen for two years from the neck of someone I'll never see again.

Who doesn't exist. Not any more.

That parcel meant the time for adventure is now.

Maya

Since we got here Dad's been jumping at every leaf twitch, every monkey screech. Looking behind him like there's a flesh-eating plant on his trail, like he was expecting something else. Someone?

Dad who isn't scared of anything.

Now I get it.

It was them. Charles and Rosa. They sent the letter. And they've got him.

Why?

I've got no idea.

But there's no way they're going to get me too.

My feet slip on the mud outside the lodge door. It rained last night. Heavy, like fistball drops smashing on to the roof. Channels are cut into the earth like canyon cracks running down to the river.

Charles grabs my arm and tries to pull me along.

I pull it back. 'I can walk by myself!'

CLICK. My brain snaps the fury in his face when I say it.

Rosa tries to steer my waist. 'Let's go.'

I dodge her hand like earwig pincers.

My eyes are blurry, the jungle heat is making me sweat.

'Drink this.' She passes me a bottle of water. It's frosty cold.

No way. What if they've drugged it?

I hold Dad's note in my hand and step out over the cracks and up on to the walkway. A Jesus lizard ducks under a rock, a bushbaby scampers up a branch.

And when we reach the end I see the canoe bobbing on the jetty at the bottom of the steps with bottle-top lids for non-slip treads.

I pull back.

Charles tries to grab me but I twist my elbow out of his hand and ram it into his throat. I swipe my pack out of Rosa's arms. Charles snatches the pack strap.

I pull.

He pulls back and his frog eyes bulge.

Two red macaws shoot out of the trees and scream.

I spit in his eye and kick him in the balls and jump off the walkway, into the arms of nature.

And run.

Raul

We set off at 4 a.m. in a van with the team and rattle along. The guys shake hands and slap each other on the back. I like how happy Dad looks when he sees them all. We hook up with the walkers out of town. Three Australians, two Americans, one French. They're nice.

I walk with the Australians at the back, up over the Dead Woman's Pass and down into the Pacaymayo Valley. They take a lot of photos – one they think's of a puma that's actually a dog and we laugh a lot. I make the most of their company. Tomorrow I'll be on my own.

We break to make camp. Ropes and canvas slide through the crew's and my hands as we pull the hikers' tents tight, looping the ropes through the pegs and stamping them into the ground against the wind. Once one lifted clean off the mountain with the sleeper still inside it. Some people say it was the wind. Others say it was the Abu, the spirit of the mountain, full of rage and throwing the tourist off the cliff.

For what?

Disrespect. The guy had left beer cans piled up by the river.

People don't disrespect Pachamama round here. Pachamama is Mother Nature – she's the earth and everything in it. Disrespect that and you disrespect yourself.

They found him downstream stuck to a rock before the falls. I guess she wanted to teach him a lesson.

They fished him out like a bag of trash. Live trash.

Dad lights the gas ring in the chef's tent and cooks up plates of *lomo saltado* – beef with onions and peppers – that sizzles and makes the tent smell like hanan pacha, Inca heaven.

All the walkers come in, their plates held high.

Simone from America stops crying on the phone to her boyfriend and Anton, the French guy, sniffs the air and grins.

The crew take theirs and slap Dad on the back.

Dad smiles. He takes pride in his food. Mami calls him *manos magicas* – magic hands – 'cos he puts sparkle into whatever he makes. Which is always something. Even though all we seem to live on back

23

home some days is air. I'd like to see how all those fancy city chefs cope on a two-ring burner on the side of a mountain.

The team have made a fire and we sit round it and fill our faces full of rice.

'Hey, Raul,' the guide next to me says.

He stares into my face.

'What?' I don't look at him.

He takes my chin in his hand, like he can see what's inside me. Like he can read my thoughts. I feel the parcel Aiko gave me in my pocket like it's red-hot. And glowing. I didn't show it to my dad. I daren't. Though it'd mean as much to him as it does to me. I can't believe the water brought it all this way. All the way up the Amazon, sucked up into the mountain and spat out into the water channel. Into our town. One thousand and sixty kilometres. Running through the water like a dog that got lost on moving day and ran to find its family in their new home.

Sometimes the past comes to haunt you.

I push the guide off.

'What's up?' Dad hands out plates of chocolate bananas and slaps my knee.

'Nothing.' I turn away.

The guide pours some beer for Pachamama into the earth, takes a sip and passes the bottle back to Dad and grins. 'Keep an eye on that one,' he says.

Dad looks worried.

I look down at my plate. I never know how much Dad knows about how I feel since we left. We talk about stuff. But mainly we say a lot with silence.

Dad sips the beer, passes it on and puts a hand on my shoulder. 'Life leads in many directions,' he says. 'Sometimes you have to pull the string of your heart and go.'

I can't look him in the eye. He knows. How does he know?

Sometimes you have to pull the string of your heart and go.

He's right. It's not a choice. Not any more.

My family knows all about going and leaving. Some things you can leave behind, like places. Some things you carry all your life.

Dad left the cloud forest when my sister Alessa died. We all did.

The way she died has never left my father.

Or me.

The guilt grows in my stomach like a sponge.

*

I think of the heat of Dad's hand on my shoulder like he's still there, when I'm standing, pack on my back in the sunrise next morning. Sun on my face, ice wind in my hair. I look back at the camp. Asleep in the mist. I look down at the moon on Rick's watch and hold Alessa's necklace in my hand.

5 a.m.

It's time to go.

Maya

I run into the jungle, a whole world of up – trees way over my head, up into the clouds. My feet slip as I run in my knee-length lodge boots. My hair flops in my face. I flick it back and follow the trail. It's safer and there's space to run. Snakes and beasts avoid it.

I put my arm round a rubber trunk and skid round the corner. I run with fear, I run with speed, I run with sweat and a bigger trust in nature and tarantulas and whatever they might throw at me than two liars I don't even know, touching my stuff and trying to shove me into a boat.

I hear them. Behind. Feet smushing through the mud.

But I'm fast. Like a cheetah.

Like a fiery Glaswegian midge screaming it down the trail.

The path splits, I go left.

Splits again. I go right.

But I am not fast enough. Charles is on my tail. My legs are shorter than his.

But I do have a brain.

I jump over a branch, skid past a woven-headed mushroom and look up.

Up.

CLICK, creepers.

CLICK, a walking palm tree with legs like stilts.

CLICK, the wide cracked roots of a ficus tree that reach into the earth like octopus tentacles sucking up soil.

I jump at the cracks, jam my foot into a hold, pull my knee high and slide my body up the trunk.

Up and up.

I pull against the wood in a wide hug. A two-toed sloth droops off a branch two body lengths up. It closes its black moon eyes and smiles. I smile back and close mine too and turn my face into the tree.

And pretend I am one.

I am a tree.

I am a tree.

I am a ...

Raul

I take out my phone and look at the text from Matias.

Tonight, he says. *It has to be tonight.*

Yeah tonight – I type and hit send.

People here might share their houses with chickens, but everyone has phones. Communication is important. People are the most important thing. I remember when I first got mine. When Uncle Carlos brought one to the forest and we thought it was magic.

I walk down over the pass, past the valley of orchids and over rock-desert dust and on to the road.

Plucked out of nature on to the man-made tarmac.

I hold up a hand to wave goodbye to the green and think of my dad rubbing his eyes and waking up to an empty space where I used to be. Cooking breakfast for the crew. I try to catch his thought wave on mine.

I'll be back. I promise.

I left a note. He'll know why I'm doing this anyway, right?

29

In his heart I know he knows.

I make a pile of rocks by the side of the road. One big one for the base, then smaller and smaller and smaller ones on top and shut my eyes. This is what we do to make wishes here. The land's alive with rock piles and hopes. We use them to connect to Mother Earth.

Matias is in the cloud forest. Miles away. There's no way I'll make it on foot.

'Bring me a car,' I whisper and I hope she's listening.

I wish it into the rocks.

'*Please* bring me a car.'

Maybe I was lucky enough to hit one of Mother Earth's entrails. 'Cos when I open my eyes I see a black Toyota rolling over the smooth tarmac ribbon that is the road. Dints in both wings. Rust on the bonnet. Heading off into the bright blue turquoise that is the sky.

Going my way.

I stick my arm out and do my best 'I am not an axe murderer' face. As the car gets closer I look into the faces in the front.

A woman, sunglasses, long fingernails, pink T-shirt is driving.

Another woman, long hair, curly, big smile is

sitting alongside.

They look like they are singing. They don't look like axe murderers either.

The car slows, the brakes squeal and they stop. They look at each other and their eyes turn into crescent moons. 'Where are you going?'

'Iquitos,' I say.

They laugh. Iquitos is hundreds of miles from here. 'Are you crazy?' The passenger leans closer, like I'm a chicken she's inspecting.

'Get in,' the driver nods. 'Let's do it!' I thank her and my lucky stone stack, and climb in before they can change their minds.

Maya

I crawl along a branch so I can hang, and look down.
Charles runs past below.

I breathe out.

'Wait!' Rosa runs behind him but stops and puts
her arms out.

Charles runs back. 'This is where the prints stop,'
she says and points at the ground.

Her forehead is dripping with sweat.

My hands are too. I start to slip and grip harder.
It makes me sweat more.

The sloth hangs easily on the next branch up,
its nails curved over the branches. Its arms free
and easy.

Be a sloth, I think. *Be a sloth.* I try to hang loose
and free.

They start to search around, like I might be
behind a bush. A bush? Nothing here grows that low.

They start to look up.

UP.

I want to chuck rocks at their heads, but all I have is leaves.

The buzz of a million invisible winged things sings in my ears. A giant beetle crawls over my leg.

I think, *If they come for me I'll bite them.*

The sun finds a chink in the canopy to cut through. It shines on my face. And glows through my hair, like someone stroking my head.

I think about what our guide said when we first got here. 'Respect the forest and the forest respects you,' he said. The sloth smiles. I relax.

And down below someone screams.

Raul

Iquitos is the city in the jungle. The furry piece of mould in a cracked piece of cheese. It isn't home, but it's near it. It's the first step.

The only way in or out is by plane. Or river.

You can't drive there. The rainforest is holding the roads off. So far. Papi Rosales says if you chopped into the forest it'd grow back twice as thick and twice as strong behind your back. And wrap its vines round your neck to say its thanks.

That or the Chullachaki will get you.

Papi Rosales is the best thing about our town. I first met him when I was sitting against the wall, flicking grit and feeling sad with nothing else to do. He sat next to me and said, 'There are two cats swimming across a river. One-two-three cat and *un-deux-trois* cat. Which one won?'

I shook my head.

'One-two-three cat,' he said. '*Un-deux-trios quatre cinq* (cat sank).'

I smiled and he smiled too, and we were friends after that. He lives three streets down. The house with the twisted wooden door and green vines that peek out over the edges. We used to sit in the garden, listening to the water running down through the town, out the mountain. Channelled by the Incas.

Sometimes when you live by something that's always running, it makes you realise how much you're standing still.

We used to sit by lanterns and I would listen to his stories in the dark, while my mother washed dishes at Koricancha and my father cooked at the Hearts café. And they both came home tired and slept while I went to school.

He used to talk about saltwater dolphins that carried women off to their underwater cities. And Chullachaki. The guardian of the forest with one backwards foot who can take on any form and lure you into the jungle so deep you can't find your way back.

I wonder where Chullachaki was when Alessa, my sister, needed him.

We used to live downriver from Iquitos. Half a day's travel by canoe.

Before Alessa died and we had to move.

Everyone moved.

Everyone except Matias. Who just plain refused.

We haven't seen each other in two years.

The driver turns the radio up higher and the music bounces off the car windows as we bounce over a rock in the road. I take Aiko's parcel out of my pocket to stop it bouncing on to the floor.

She smiles. 'I'm Diane.'

'And Elena.' The other girl turns.

'Raul,' I say and look at the floor, hoping that's all they'll ask.

'Where is your father?' Elena says.

'Working.'

'And your mother?'

'Same.'

They talk to each other about their mothers and don't expect any input from me, which is a relief. 'I dreamt a bird dropped a stone into my hand last night,' Diane says and taps the wheel.

I clutch the parcel.

'A condor?' Her friend raises an eyebrow.

'A vulture,' she says and I meet her eyes in the mirror.

Vultures are birds of death. I grip the parcel.

'I think that stone was you,' she says to me.

I look away. I wonder if I have the smell of death about me.

'I'll take you to the airport in Aguas Calientes,' she nods.

'Thanks,' I say and grip the seat with my other hand.

'That's miles out,' Elena grins and turns the radio up higher. 'Your heart's bigger than your head,' she says. 'Your heart's bigger than a Big Mac and fries.'

They both grin, and the music shimmies and the sun shines off Diane's dark shiny hair through the window.

We drive to Aguas Calientes, the town of hot springs. It's the nearest place with an airport.

Diane and Elena talk about their lives, their boyfriends, and I try not to listen.

We wind up the pass and the road rubbernecks on itself. As we snap round a corner we see a rent-a-van fallen off the road, drifting down the mountain on the scree on its side. Diane crosses herself and sucks in a breath.

The passengers stand in the middle of nowhere, talking on their phones.

37

Diane brakes and she yells out the window. 'You want a hand?'

'It's OK.' A man in orange flip-flops waves at us. 'My uncle's coming.'

Three vultures circle.

'You sure?' Diane squints.

'Sure, sure,' the man yells.

The van slides. And I think it's funny how life's like that. It can just flip you over like a pancake when you're not expecting it.

'That happens all the time here.' Diane has sad eyes. 'That could be us.'

'But it isn't.' Elena spreads her fingers and her bracelets jingle. We drive on. A bright song comes on and the music shakes the darkness off. Elena claps her hands and sings and shimmies.

Diane hides her smile behind her hand. 'Where are you from?' she asks me.

'Ollantaytambo.'

Diane swerves to avoid a double-loaded onion truck swinging wide around the corner. We're already a long way from Ollantaytambo.

When we get to the airport Diane gets out. It's funny

how you can feel like friends with someone you've only known for two hours. She pats my arm and smiles.

I thank her and get my Coke can of cash out. Three hundred sols – that's ninety dollars. I know it from the walkers who tip in dollars. Diane waves the money away. 'My grandpapi lives in Ollantaytambo,' she says and hands me my bag.

Elena honks the horn and she gets in.

We wave and pull faces as they drive off.

And I enter the big glass sliding doors swallowing air that's like the sols in my pocket.

Light.

Fresh.

Crispy.

And not enough to fly on.

Maya

The scream comes from Rosa.

I look down and see the sky is raining on her. And Charles. Not water, but light. Light like snow.

Soft. Round. Glowing and falling from the trees like gold dust.

It's raining light balls.

The balls hiss and scorch as they touch the earth. Disappearing when they land, like bubbles. Bouncing on to the bodies of the two sweaty kidnappers, who try to dance out of their way, but can't.

The balls keep coming.

Soft and gentle.

Falling and hissing, like coal dropping in ice.

Burning the kidnappers.

Rosa screams, Charles roars.

Me and the sloth look down and smile.

'Go on, light!' I whisper. 'Go on!'

Raul

I walk into the airport and take my rucksack off. A bottle top sticks out the top. Inca Kola. The drink of the gods. I lift it up. A roll of cash falls out too. Diane must have put it there. Diane and Elena are angels.

I check out the departure board and walk over to the flight desk. It's so red and shiny I feel like running my tongue over the edge. But I don't. The woman behind it stares at me.

'How much is a ticket for Iquitos?'

'For today?'

I nod.

She taps into the computer. 'Eight hundred and seventy sol.'

I don't think Mum and Dad even earn that in a year.

'You want one?' She looks at me and I back away, looking at the floor.

'No.' I shuffle back. 'Thank you.' I'll have to find another way.

41

My phone buzzes and I pull it out. It's Matias.

How long? he says.

I don't know, I type.

It has to be tonight, he says.

I know, I reply and shove it back in my pocket. The phone bangs into Aiko's parcel like a reminder and I shudder.

Entry to Iquitos is plane or boat only. Canoe from here takes weeks. I can't paddle that long. I don't have that long. I don't have a canoe anyway.

I could stow away on a plane? I imagine falling out of the wheel arch and splatting on the tarmac. Or getting arrested. No way I'm doing that either.

Sometimes things take more planning than you think.

I should've planned this better.

I'm stuck.

I put my trust in the gods. I put my fate in faith.

Something bangs into me from behind and I turn round.

'Hey!' I yell, and see a pile of delivery boxes on wheels. I see a head with a smile behind the boxes. A big grin. Waving at me. 'Raul?' the head yells.

No way. I clutch my pocket and wonder what kind

of magic Aiko's dad put on that parcel.

'Omar?'

He skids round the boxes and hugs me like a bear.

Dad and Omar have been friends since I can remember. When we left the jungle we went together. My family, Omar's family. We travelled in the same truck. Cut out of the trees and into the city. We stuck together and tried to turn the pain of what we'd lost into something new.

Dad and Omar used to work together when we first came to the Sacred Valley and Dad had to shoe shine before he got a job as a cook. Earning one sol a shoe.

One sol. Not even enough for a bag of *cancha chulpe*.

They earned a little, laughed a lot and we all squashed into a one-room apartment. I remember the first time we turned on a hot tap together and squealed at the magic. Omar's grandma refused to use it. His grandad got into the bath and grinned.

Omar used to come home after work and do the chicken dance with us and made us laugh till snot came out of our noses. Then he moved on and so did we and we haven't seen each other since.

Till now.

'What you doing here?' we say and slap each other.

'Where's your papi?' he says.

'Work.'

'Your mami?'

'Home.'

He raises his eyebrows.

'It's complicated.' I look at my feet. I can't tell him what I'm doing. He'll say it's stupid. He'll say it's dangerous. 'You delivering boxes now?' I kick my foot on the lino.

'Kinda.' He grips my shoulder tight. 'It's so good to see you.'

I want to ask him how he lives with what happened to us. It's something we don't talk about, not at my house. Not ever. We just get on, and the pain swells inside us till one day I think we're going to explode.

'You sure grew up quick, Raul.' He whistles and shakes my hand, and then we have to wheel his boxes out of the way of two people in big hats and the security guard who's yelling at us.

'I did some changing too.' He grabs the handles and smiles at me. 'I went to college.'

'Seriously?'

'Seriously. I'm a pilot.'

'No way.'

'Way.'

I grin and look down at the box on the top of his stack.

'H. Anderson,' it says. 'El Dorado Hotel, Plaza de Armas, Iquitos.'

Iquitos!

I nearly jump out of my shorts.

Maya

The sloth blinks and turns its head at one mile an hour for a better view. We've got the best seats in the house up here.

In the trees, animals crawl to the edges of branches, gathering together, looking down in wonder. The light balls keep falling.

Opposite us two furry things hug each other, peering out of the canopy. Out of the dark.

The small one screeches and tries to touch a ball and pulls its arm back and jumps on to the belly of its mother.

All week I've heard these guys, but I haven't seen them. Now here we all are. Together. The forest doesn't let the fire touch us. Not a ball drops on anyone but Charles and Rosa, who turn and run. We hear the trails of their screams like music bouncing over the leaves.

Until they're so far away it stops.

Me and the sloth hang in chirruping, buzzing

silence. Its moon eyes shine. I pull myself round the branch and sit up. Beetles' feelers droop over the edge of leaves, tasting the atmosphere. Frogs sit and stare at each other. And out of the blue, a howler monkey screams in my ear and I scream.

And slip.

And fall.

Badly.

Raul

'Got room for one more?' I look up at him and grin.

'For you?' Omar looks me over.

I nod.

'Your butt's got big but not that big,' he says and smiles and does the chicken dance right there in the middle of the airport. I could hug him. We laugh, but are pushed on by the security guard who has a gun and no sense of humour.

'You going home?' I ask him. Hoping he might be and I don't have to do this alone.

'Nah, I just go for business. How about you? You going home, *chico*?' he says and his eyebrows meet in the middle.

'Kind of.' I look away. 'You ever go back?'

'No. I don't want to see it. I keep my memories in here.' He taps his head. 'What's past is past. Nothing new there I care to see.'

We wheel his parcels out the door and over to a white two-seater with red wings and one propeller.

I've never been in a plane before. Never wanted to. 'How long you been a pilot?'

'You don't trust me?' Omar grins and waves at a guy in orange overalls. 'Your papi knows you're here, right?'

'Sort of.'

'Sort of how?'

'I left a note.'

He gets out his phone. 'I'm ringing your papi.'

'Don't. Please. I'm going to help Matias, all right? He needs me.'

'Matias?'

'Yeah.'

'Why?' His phone hovers halfway to his ear.

'He needs help. He said if I didn't come I'd regret it for the rest of my life.' I don't say I've got enough regrets already. There isn't space for any more. I hang my head and don't look him in the eye.

The guy in orange overalls starts yelling at Omar and waving his arms. Omar yells back and throws his arms over his head. 'OK, OK,' he says and slams the hold door shut. 'Let's go.'

We climb into the cockpit and strap ourselves in.

Omar puts headphones over my ears. 'For the

noise,' he yells and starts the engine. My stomach and my teeth vibrate. I can't believe we're going up in the sky in this. The doors feel as thin as a tuna tin. We wheel along the tarmac and my knuckles go white from clenching.

'Relax, *chico*.' Omar pats my back.

I try to unhunch my shoulders. They stay by my ears.

The plane bumps along the runway.

Omar looks out the windscreen. My eyes are wide. The buildings and the mountains speed by. Everything turns to blur and we lift up.

Maya

I land.

Badly.

When I wake up it's dark.

My face is tangled up in brown bits that turn out to be roots. I'm in the base of the tree.

A voice is calling.

Pain is screaming down my leg.

The voice lifts my head up.

It's light again.

I look into a face with long brown floppy hair. Brown skin. Not the frog guy. Younger. A face that seems happy in the trees. With no shoes on. He has a vest that was white once and a monkey with small green eyes on his shoulder. The monkey screams at me and runs away.

'You fell out of the ficus tree,' the face says. 'You're probably cursed. Or diseased.'

The sloth looks down and smiles.

'Light balls fell out of the sky,' I say.

'That's nice,' he says, and lifts me out of the roots and over his shoulder.

My arms hang down his back. The leg pain makes my head buzz.

His shorts light up.

'Your phone is ringing.'

'Yes.'

'Aren't you going to answer it?'

'No.'

Who are you?'

'I am Matias,' he says.

'That's nice,' I say, and then the pain makes everything go black again.

Raul

We land bouncily and I throw up.

I chuck my clothes in the bin of the airport toilet and get out my only clean set and wash my face.

And ring Matias.

There's no answer.

It's typical. Matias is older than me and lives alone. He lives how he wants, does what he wants. He likes to think he's the boss. No one can make Matias do anything.

We've hung out since forever. 'Cos he was older, he looked out for us in the forest. He looked out for everyone. We used to play round his house and he taught me scorpion kicks, and Alessa and him played hide-and-seek. 'Cept he wasn't Matias any more when we played like that. He was the Mapinguari – the forest spirit ogre with a turtle shell and big green Cyclops eye. Alessa used to run under the house. Shrieking so loud the rats ran out.

Omar bangs on the door. 'You OK?'

'No.' I come out.

'I'm sorry, man.' He slaps me on the back. The heat is thick and heavy. I stand by an air fan and let the cold blow over my head. When it catches the water it's like an ice fountain on my face. The cold is delicious. We wheel the parcels through the airport.

'You want me to retake my exams?' Omar says.

I smile.

'When I was learning I used to chuck up every day,' he says.

'Really?'

'Nah.' He smiles. 'It'll pass.'

'It better. This is my last shirt.' I roll my eyes.

He opens his bag and slips me a clean shirt out of sight. Way too big. But good. At least it'll stop me from stinking after a couple of days. 'Thanks, Omar.' I open the bottle of Inca Kola from Diane and it sprays all over the floor. I dance it out the way of my trousers and drink the fizz out the top.

It's the best. Like yellow ice cream with bubbles.

Omar looks round the airport like he's searching for someone.

'Matias is upriver,' I say. 'He won't come into town.'

'Same old Matias,' he sighs.

I nod. We stand there for a minute drinking in the heat, looking out the door. 'Do you miss it?' I say. 'The way things were.'

'Back home?' He puts a hand on my shoulder, slow, like someone at a funeral. I nod. 'Yeah,' he says. 'I miss it. I miss it every day. You want to know a secret?'

'Like what?' My head's so full of secrets I don't think I've got space for any more.

'When I'm up there, looking down, I talk to it,' he whispers.

'The forest?'

'Yeah. I ask it to forgive me for not sticking up for the trees. For not being there.'

'It wasn't your fault we had to leave,' I say.

'It wasn't yours either,' he says.

I look at the floor.

He sighs. 'I tell it about my life now. What's going on. Sounds strange, huh?'

I shake my head. No, it doesn't. The forest's deep in all of us and no one can take it out. Like if you cut us open there'd be coils of it in our stomachs, like we're part of each other. 'Does it talk back?'

He laughs. 'Nah,' he says. 'Don't you think that's kinda rude?'

Actually, I think it's probably best. I think if it could talk back it'd be screaming.

'Can I get a lift in with the parcels?'

'Sure,' he says, and dodges a woman freaking out at a spider.

'Thanks, Omar.' I dodge the spider too and we wheel the boxes out through the doors into the thick jungle heat.

We look at each other and shut our eyes and breathe deep.

'Feels good, right?' he says and from his voice I know he's smiling.

'Yeah,' I say, and I feel like the cloud forest's pouring clouds back into my lungs. Till the DHL van comes and pumps out diesel.

Omar goes to ask the guy to take me as a special delivery and we do our made-up handshake and he helps me into the back and passes me the parcel for Eldorado Hotel. 'Hold this for me, *chico.*'

'Sure,' I nod and sit on a crate in the corner.

'Keep in touch with me, right?' he says and we swap numbers. 'Let me know when you need me. If stuff gets . . .'

'What?'

'Serious.'

We know serious. We've seen it. We've seen what's out there.

I know the kinds of things he means and wish I didn't.

'Just ring and let me know you're OK. OK?' he says.

'OK,' I nod.

And Omar's smile becomes a face in the crack in the door, and then darkness as the door is slammed and I bounce off to Plaza de Armas.

Maya

I wake up on a table in a tin-roof hut with a wooden floor and a creature that looks like a half rabbit, half weasel with teeny ears, sitting up on its back legs staring at me.

I try to stroke it and it leaps off the table on to a workbench and starts hitting my boots with a pencil.

I look down at my feet. My boots must've been taken off and laid out there.

One ankle has been strapped up in a bandage and the blood has been cleaned off my legs. Scratches run down from my knees and I feel an egg on my elbow swelling into a big blue bruise.

A head pops up from under the table.

I scream.

'Hi, I'm Matias.' The head climbs out and becomes a person.

I stare at him.

'Last time we met you were delirious and tried to bite my arm.' He points at his elbow.

Matias. Right. I remember. Sort of. I don't remember the biting part.

I sit up and fold my arms.

Is he one of the bad guys? Is he keeping me here for them? My heart beats.

I look round the hut for weapons or an escape route.

CLICK. I see that the wooden floor leads out to an open-sided veranda. Criss-crossed wood makes a balcony and a wall between the hut and the outside.

CLICK. I see a door carved out of the wood at the back of the shack on the left.

Creepers hang by a long open window. A blue bird with a beak that looks way too big swings on a branch and flies down.

We're not on the ground.

We're high up.

On a platform.

He looks at my leg and smiles. 'You can't jump from here.'

I grab my boot and hold it over his head. The creature attacks the other one. 'Who are you? Are you one of them?'

'Who?'

I wave the boot and my arms to try and get the words out. 'The people who kidnapped my dad.'

'They kidnapped your dad?' Matias walks over to a stool made from a tree trunk and sits. 'That's news to me.'

'You know him?'

He nods.

I look hard at his face. Try and work out if he's one of the guys from the lodge and I just didn't notice. 'How?'

'I just do.' The creature stops attacking the boot and runs on to his knee and chirrups.

'What is that?'

'An Agouti paca.' Matias scratches between his ears. 'I call him Steven.'

'That?' I point at a bowl and arrangement of leaves. The leaves go all around the table. Where my head was.

'They're soaking up your curse.'

'I'm not cursed.'

'Not any more.' Matias shrugs. 'Ficus trees usually curse or disease people. It takes a while to wear off.'

I remember the beliefs our guide taught us. About the powers of trees and the spirits who guard them.

About stilt walkers who walk through the forest at night. And lupuna trees whose mothers hide in their bellies and get revenge for disrespect if you so much as wee on them.

I look at the workbench piled up with pencils and notebooks. Piles and piles of books.

Steven runs on to the table and nicks one of my leaves and runs out the door screeching.

Matias picks up a glass off the bench. 'Drink this.'

'What is it?'

'Water.'

'Oh.'

I thought it might be some sort of potion. I look at his face. His eyes are smiling. His fringe is floppy. He doesn't look like one of them. But how can you tell? I trusted Dad till he disappeared. And he's meant to be the person I trust most in the world.

If I need to rely on strangers I'm grateful I found one. Though really he found me. I wiggle my toes and appreciate the bandage and that I'm not lying with my head stuck in a tree root. 'Sorry I bit you.'

'It's OK, I'm used to biters,' he says, and lifts a tarantula off a shelf and puts it out the door. It scuttles off after a bird.

'Why'd you rescue me?'

'You looked like a dead sloth.' He hangs his arms down like one and laughs. 'I don't leave things to die.' He shrugs. 'Unless they want it.'

'You don't know anything about what I want.'

He pulls up on to the bench. His legs hang down.

'I know lots about you,' he says. 'You are Maya Anderson. Daughter of Handi Anderson, the Light Man. You like PG Tips tea and cheese.

'And I know the people who are hunting you.

'I'm hunting them myself.'

Raul

The van rolls around the streets and I bounce in the back with the cardboard boxes. I stick my legs out to the sides to stop me sliding too far. I try and guess what's in the parcel and feel it like a New Year present. 'Cept they're obvious. Everyone here gives each other yellow pants at New Year. It doesn't feel like pants.

We stop and the driver opens the door. I take his hand and hop out, and give him the parcel. He winks and nods, and wheels them all away like patients into a hospital. I watch it go inside with the others and disappear into the crowd.

The plaza is full of people. I push past women with orchids higher than their heads strapped to their backs, kids selling llama pencils, a blind man making music with seashells.

I drink more Inca Kola and buy two empanadas from a street seller on the corner, then walk down through the town to the harbour. I need a boat to get to Matias. There's no other way of getting in jungle that deep.

I ask three guys with canoes if they're going upriver. They shake their heads.

I walk along and see a banana boat. Low in the water, piles of green bananas loaded in mountains.

'You going upriver?'

The driver folds his arms and nods.

'How much?'

'Fifty sols.' He chews a coca leaf and squints in the sun.

'Fifteen.'

'Thirty.'

'Twenty.'

'OK.' He rocks his head from side to side. I hand him the cash, get in and sit at the back. If there's spiders coming out of those bananas I don't want them on me. My brother once put a spider down my shirt when I was eight. Now I hate spiders.

The man starts the engine and we speed along the river.

I wonder why Matias hasn't rung. I can't do this without him.

I think about Omar talking to the jungle and I make wishes to it, under the sound of the engine.

And get out my phone.

And ring.

AGAIN.

Maya

Matias's blue shorts light up as his phone buzzes in his pocket. He pulls it out and starts speaking in Spanish.

I don't know Spanish. Not much anyway beyond:

cheese – *queso*.

and thank you – *gracias*.

He puts the phone back in his pocket and hands me a banana.

'If you're hungry, eat this,' he says, and walks out. 'Keep your head down and out of the ficus trees and don't even think about touching my books,' he yells over his shoulder. 'I'll be back.' He jumps off the veranda and vanishes.

Steven follows.

'Hey!' I sit up and eat the banana. And shuffle myself over to the edge of the table and grab two more out of the wooden bowl on the bench and eat those too. I'm starving.

Steven runs in and grabs one and runs off again.

I pull myself over the edge of the table and lower my body down on to the floor with my arms. I put my bad foot on the floor and wish I hadn't. Pain shoots up my leg and nearly makes me sick all the bananas out.

I shuffle and hop along on my good foot over to the workbench and the books.

I pick up a book.

In the corner a radio crackles into life and I jump like I just set off a trap. Is Matias going to come flying in? No. He doesn't.

Music fills the hut and late afternoon sunbeams bounce off the roof. The sun's hit the solar panel on the radio and set it off.

I open the book. It's filled with pencil drawings. And Spanish writing. It doesn't say 'cheese' or 'thank you'.

I flip through and run my fingers over the diagrams of trees. Intricate drawings. Done with love. And meticulous attention.

I try to sound out the names of the trees.

Wimba. So tall it goes off the page. So wide the monkey he's drawn next to it looks like a flea.

Lupuna. With roots like snakes.

Árbol estrangulador. The strangler fig. With branches like arms that grow out of another tree's trunk

OK, so Matias likes trees. That's kinda nice.

I turn the pages and smile till I see one about me. 'Maya Anderson.'

Steven runs over, grabs the notebook out of my hands and screeches into the corner.

'You'd look if it was you!' I yell at him. 'If he knew stuff about your life, you'd want to know why!'

We stare at each other. I go to grab the book back. Steven barks – *back off* – like a little dog.

And out of nowhere a light ball pops out of my rucksack by the door and scurries along the floor. It's round and glowing. And leaving a scorch mark trail on the wood. Me and Steven stare at it. Steven's fur prickles and his hackles go up. It grows a bit like a plump baby rabbit that shines and is see through. Smoke drifts up behind it and heat shimmers round it like a halo. Two eyes pop out and look back at me, shy and a bit embarrassed. Then it jumps off the edge of the veranda and disappears.

Raul

The banana boat drops me at the jetty cut into the mud. The driver spits out the coca leaf and nods. We shake hands.

I climb out on to the wooden steps cut into the earth. The boat pulls away and I remember the day we left. Boatloads of us up and down in one canoe. Arms full of what we had, which wasn't much. Mainly each other.

I remember all of us standing on the shore. Everyone was stiff. And fear hung off us. Jaguars could smell it for miles. We waited for our turn. No other choice. Having to leave and wanting to stay. Torn away from home like babies off their mothers' bellies.

'Cept we weren't screeching.

Hardly anyone said anything. We were stepping out into something new. Scattering out like it would never be the same again.

It wasn't.

A capybara slides into the water with a bird on its

head. I've missed their big wide noses, little ears and beady eyes. I've missed stroking their fluffy heads. I used to have a pet one called Narizo – that means nose – as it kept twitching it. It hung around outside our house every morning and I fed it and it let me tickle its whiskers. I watch this one swim away.

I wonder what to say to Matias. I wonder what he looks like now.

If he'll notice my moustache fluff.

I breathe in the green heat that's so alive it feels like it might start growing things inside my towny-boy lungs, and head off up the steps.

Matias should be waiting at the top.

He isn't.

Maya

I lean over the balcony and look for the light-ball creature. And see nothing.

The jungle keeps on buzzing.

And squawking.

And screeching.

Nothing moves. 'Cept Steven. Who chucks the book under the cupboard and runs over to me. Strange things happen in the jungle. Maybe I am cursed?

I think Steven's going to bite me, but he rubs his head into my arm.

'Don't ask me what that was,' I say, and stare at the scorch trail on the floor. 'I have no idea.'

Steven's nose is warm and soft, and I like the feeling of his breathing against my skin. His head burrows deeper into my elbow.

'I wish you were my cat,' I say and stroke his head. 'No offence.'

Steven chunters and chitters.

Back home Socks always makes everything OK. Socks makes everything feel better. Sometimes the world has a way of making you feel very alone. When Dad works. When he shuts me out. When no one's around. But I never feel like that with Socks. When my nose is pressed into his fur.

I think about Matias spying on us.

On me.

Why?

If Steven trusts him, I trust him. Don't I?

Do you really trust a person who even notices you like cheese?

I scratch between Steven's ears and he closes his eyes and chatters. Then runs off inside and hides under the cupboard. I pull myself along on my butt and lie on my side, sticking my hand under, grabbing the book he dropped there. He starts to screech.

'It's about me, right?' I say. 'I'm only looking at stuff about me.'

Steven turns away and hunches.

I sit up and flip through to my section. It's the last bit in the book. So new the ink's smudged like it never properly dried before he shut it. I wonder if that's what he was doing under the table.

Maya Anderson. It says a load of stuff I don't understand. I turn the page to a picture of me. In the tree. Light balls falling out of the sky. I see me hanging next to the sloth. The sloth looks great. My hair hangs wild and free. The lines are beautiful.

I freak out and slam the book shut.

He was there?

Where was he? Hiding in a bush and waiting for me to fall out?

Where is he now?

Steven snatches the book back. I let it go and crawl out of the hut and on to the veranda.

I look out on to a ghost town. Wooden houses, overgrown and abandoned, standing with their doors and windows open like mouths gaping. Vines grow thick over the windows, clinging to their stilt legs. Empty. They're all empty.

Some of the roof timbers are missing, but what they're really missing is people.

I look down and see a firepit and a half-built canoe resting on wooden supports. A garden cleared out of the forest. Plants carefully tended. Rows of things growing, sprouting out of the thick red earth. It seems weird next to all the emptiness. Life and order. Emptiness and chaos. Like this house is keeping something going that died ages ago.

The trees are silent and full of eyes and wings.

I have to get out of here.

'What's the best way out of this place?' I say, and Steven hops up and chucks himself off the balcony. The last thing I see of him is his tail.

'Eeeeeeeeeee,' he squeals. And thuds into the mud.

I shuffle to the edge and look over.

Two bright blue butterflies the size of handprints take off from the handrail.

On one side of the veranda there's a rope hanging. I could slide down it on one leg and find a stick for a crutch at the bottom.

I look at the scorch mark the fireball creature made in the leaves.

I look around. It's nowhere to be seen.

A mantis stares at me.

'What?' I say. 'Did you see it too?'

It scuttles off. I don't know what reply I expect from a mantis.

I pull myself up and grab my boots off the bench.

I stick them over my feet and push-slide myself backwards over to the rope. It's a long drop down.

My legs hang over the edge. I reach out, grab it with both hands and slide.

OW!

Raul

I sit and wait. The hours click round on Rick's watch.

The banana boat heads back to town. Empty.

'Where is he?' I say to the trees. Nothing answers.

The trees probably know though. The day we left, Matias disappeared into them and refused to come out.

His family went crazy. Screaming, crying, cajoling him.

Then they left. They had to. The pickup was waiting for them at the other end, like for all of us. Our first time in any kind of car. We sat in the back with our feet bouncing, squashed together like sticks in a bundle. Our soles tingling with their first taste of tarmac.

Matias's family found work in Belen. The floating city in Iquitos. Matias's uncle, Carlos, sorted it the way he sorted most things. He was our contact with the outside world. In the forest when we needed stuff we couldn't make, he brought it. That's how it worked.

Carlos and his mum came back to look for him and found Matias in the house refusing to leave.

'It is as it is,' his mum said.

They decided to check in on him at weekends and he became the eyes and ears of the forest. I used to worry about him on his own. But he started hanging out at the jungle lodge most nights. Then him and Uncle Carlos joined the EIA – an underground environmental alliance – working in secret, desperate for revenge. He changed after that. After he found something to channel his anger into. And he hasn't been alone since then. He's just been desperate to drag me into it. Which he hasn't. Till now.

Till he texted to say if I didn't come I'd regret it for the rest of my life. He's always been overdramatic.

But my heart knows it's true. Once some things are changed they can't go back to the way they were. Ever.

I eat the empanadas and lie on the wood and my brain pulls me into a thick heavy sleep.

When I wake up it's dark. And raining.

Maya

The forest floor is alive with crawling things. I watch millipedes longer than my arms rippling along, and fasten down my sleeves. I butt-shuffle myself over to the canoe and pull up to standing. I brush ants and beetles and a curious spider off my trousers, then reach into the bottom of the boat and lift the paddle out and put it under my armpit.

Now I have a crutch. Perfect.

I follow Matias's footprints into the jungle.

It starts to rain. Not perfect.

Big fat drops patter down from the tallest trees, getting sucked up into roots. The leaves reach out like tongues desperate to be the one to catch it first.

Every so often I whisper 'Matias' into the trees, just in case he's there. I feel a bit ridiculous.

The ground gets slippy. The tracks melt into the mud and disappear. Great.

A soggy-looking Steven trots along next to me with sad eyes. His fur prickles.

'I'm not going back,' I say. 'I'm not.'

He puts his head down and looks away.

The trail ahead leads off in three different directions. I have no idea which way to go.

OK.

It's OK.

It's OK that my leg is burning and making me feel sick.

It's OK I don't have food.

I can survive on bananas. If the monkeys can find them, I can.

I wipe the water trails off my face. So what if I don't have water. I can cup my hands and catch it.

I'm not thirsty. I won't be thirsty for hours.

Yeah, it's getting dark. That's fine. Who doesn't like dark.

Everything is great. Right.

I wipe my eyes with the back of my hand and feel like collapsing on the floor and crying 'cos the pain's so bad. I want to go back to our lodge. I want to find our guide. And get help.

'Cept I can't, can I? That's the first place the kidnappers will look. That's the first place they'll be waiting for me. And then what?

Out of the dark a ping-pong ball of light shoots out and darts behind a tree.

I look at Steven. 'You see that?'

He looks up at me with big eyes.

'Hello!' I whisper and flick my head round the tree. The light ball shoots round the other side and tucks itself under a leaf. It thinks it's hiding but it leaves a trail of light like a sparkler. Plus the leaf is smoking.

'I can see you, you know.' I lift the leaf and try to touch it.

Two eyes pop on to its face and it hisses at me like a cross owl.

'Ow!' I pull back.

It floats closer and looks sorry.

Steven runs off squealing.

And out of the dark something charges at me and knocks me into a tree.

Raul

Me and Matias became brothers when my sister, Alessa, died. Blood brothers. We cut our thumbs and put them together and made a pact. You don't break trust like that. I grip Aiko's parcel in my pocket. He should be here to meet me.

But he isn't.

I need to find him. Before it gets dark.

Not this kind of dark – hazy and shadow-shifty. The proper 'can't see your hand in front of your face' kind.

I wipe the rain off my face and kick off my shoes. Jungle people don't wear shoes. Shoes don't have nerve endings – they're like going around in blindfolds. I put them in my pack, put my pack on my back and head off into the jungle.

It's been two years, but I still know the way. Once the jungle's in you, it doesn't leave you. Right?

I name the trees as I walk. Kinda like seeing old friends. 'Hey,' I say to them. The raindrops fall hard and drip softly. I hear them all around like someone throwing rice on a tin roof. It makes me smile. I round the bend and meet a bunch of tapirs who grunt at me with their long soft snouts and run off to sit in mud.

I think about Papi Rosales's stories. The Yanapuma, the devil's puma, and Chullachaki, guardian spirit of the forest who can take any form and appear anywhere. The forest spirits float round my brain like they're close, sensing I'm here and pulling in. The dark presses up against my face. I squint and my walk turns into a run.

The forest closes up around the trail like a black wax seal. It's too dark to even see where I've come from.

My heart speeds.

I run faster.

Hard buzzing balls of insects fly at my face, green thorns reach for my arms.

My feet take over.

I run like a frilled lizard, pumping my arms like a howler monkey.

The path splits into three. My head turns and disconnects from my feet which skid. I slide.

Screech-slipping, like a rat down a drainpipe, and crash into something solid. With a stick.

That screams.

Maya

The charging thing knocks me into a tree. I hit out with my paddle and scream.

Sometimes noise is power. That's why lions roar, right?

I scream till my lungs sting and hold my paddle out like a sword. If it comes near me again I'll knock it out. No way I'm dying here in the dark eaten by a beast.

'Back off!' I yell.

It doesn't. It pushes me so I bounce off the tree.

The light ball peeks out, flashes round the trunk and lights up the air between us like a laser.

I see it isn't a beast. It's a boy.

Getting jumped on from behind. By Matias.

The boy's knees buckle and they fall on to the floor. Matias gets his arm round the boy's neck and the boy shouts something. Matias screams and I hit them both with the paddle to make them stop and fall back into the tree.

Raul

Before I can see what I crashed into, something jumps on my back. I spin round to shake it off, my elbow in its throat.

'Hey, townie!'

'Matias!'

He puts a hand over my eyes and I push it off and shove him down into the mud. He gets my leg and pulls and we both go down. He gets his elbow round my throat and I bite him a bit to get free and breathe.

He screams.

The thing I crashed into hits us both with the stick and passes out.

'Ow!' I grab my jaw and look at Matias. His face lights up, goes dark and lights up again. 'Your face looks weird.' I poke his cheek.

He puts his hands on my head and turns it to look. I see the tree. I see the thing. The thing is a girl. In the toe tree?

My stomach lurches.

I pull back and hold my arms up. I don't want to touch it. Or her.

A yellow light is cocooning her body. Pulsing and throbbing. She's glowing.

Nothing moves. The whole forest is watching.

The rain patters around us. The drops hiss softly when they touch the glow.

Matias reaches out towards her.

I pull his arm back.

'Meet Maya,' he whispers.

'You know her?'

'Shh.' He pulls away and cups his other hand over my mouth and reaches into the glow. It glimmers, then parts and shrinks away like burning plastic.

'Does she usually glow?' I say through his fingers.

'No,' he says, and lifts her up over his shoulder. 'Last time she made light balls fall out of the sky.'

Raul

'Where were you?' I flick both Matias's ears for being late. And he can't hit me back or he'll drop the girl.

'Rescuing her,' he says. 'You were fine on your own. Right?' He kicks my leg and I collapse his with my knee. He keeps walking.

'I think she was finer if she can make fireballs and glow.'

'She doesn't know she glows,' Matias says.

The darkness pulls in and dances in our faces. Fluttering in and out with the moon as the clouds fly by. Letting us see things and then not. A branch slaps me in the face.

'I wish she was glowing now.'

'Call this dark, townie?' he says and trips over a stump.

We carry her through the rain. As we get closer to the village the trees open out and we see the shadow outlines of the stilt houses, and my stomach churns. I don't want to look at them. It's like looking at ghosts. My old self. My old life.

Memories creep out of the shadows and run out at me in the dark with their arms up.

I keep my head down and walk past it all like it's breathing down my neck. We climb up the back steps into Matias's house and lie the girl on the table. I look up and around, trace my hand on the wood, breathe the old smells in.

'You OK?' Matias arranges Maya's legs.

I shrug. No. Not really.

He takes off Maya's boots and checks out her ankle, which is bandaged.

I run my hand along a stack of Matias's books.

'Don't touch that,' he says and pushes me and picks one up off the floor. He dusts it on his shirt, puts it back on the pile and frowns. I push him back and he pulls out of the way and grins. 'Too slow, kerango,' he says and jumps over the balcony down to the firepit.

It feels good to be back in the forest though. To be back in green. Trees feel more forgiving than people. I jump down to the firepit too and we light a fire and make plantain and rice. Like we used to, when our

88

mums were busy with other stuff and each other. Proper jungle food.

'What's the caterpillar on your face, brother?' Matias says and stirs the silver steel pot over the fire. I stroke my moustache stubble and smile. 'You getting old, man.' He ruffles my hair.

I fix my eyes on the fire, avoiding the silhouettes of the other houses. Trying not to piece together what was there before. Or who. I don't know how Matias does it. It's like the past's sat hunched behind me, like a silent monkey. Waiting for me to turn round and remember.

'Why'd you put her on the table?'

'The floor's wood.' He serves the food out into three bowls. 'What if she glows and sets the place on fire? I'm not risking it.'

'The table's wood.'

'If the table catches fire I can throw it out the door,' he says and jump-pulls himself up on to the veranda with both hands.

'Fair enough.' I pass the bowls up and try to jump-pull up too, and fall flat on my back. My fingers just slip off. It's been too long. Jungle me is fading.

Matias leans over and laughs so hard I think he'll wet himself.

I take the back stairs.

Matias is still laughing when I go in.

He lights the kerosene lamps and does an impression of me falling off like a loose monkey. 'Townie,' he says and passes me a bowl.

I take my shirt off and wring it out the back door. The rain's thudding so hard on the roof the lamps are shaking.

It'll do what it always does here. Rain like a tap's been left on and then stop like nothing ever happened and turn to mist that rises into clouds and turns us into the cloud forest.

I go back in. The damp mists off my shorts in trails.

I look at the girl.

'She's Scottish.' Matias eats his food like he hasn't eaten all week. 'And alone.'

That makes two of us.

'You eat like a wild dog,' I say. I guess that's how you eat when you live alone and no one's around or watching. He ignores me. 'Why's she here?' I eat a spoonful and feel the heat sliding down inside.

'The same reason you are.'

I nearly drop the bowl.

'Life's complicated, *chico*,' he says and then she sits up.

Maya

I wake up back in the hut. On the table. Rain hammering on the tin roof.

My leg is twice as painful and my hand's hurting. And my armpit.

I squint at the fire flickering off lamps hanging from the ceiling, pushing the dark out the door. Matias and the boy stare at each other. Then me.

I sit up and grab a boot. 'Who are you?' I yell at the boy. 'Are you one of them?'

'No.' Matias takes the boot and puts it down. 'He's with us.'

Since when did we become an us?

Maybe since he keeps rescuing me?

I look at the boy. In the lamplight and not running, he looks much friendlier. And less like a beast. He's stroking Steven's head and a bruise is coming up on his cheek. He looks about my age. Brown skin, black hair, no shoes.

His eyes look smiley but sad.

Like there's something in them that says, *don't touch*. Something he doesn't want to look at himself.

I wonder what I look like and am glad there's no mirrors.

'Sorry,' I say. 'About hitting you.'

'*De nada*,' he says (it's nothing) and starts eating whatever's in his bowl.

I look around the table for leaves. 'Am I cursed again?'

'No.' Matias smiles and sits up on the bench next to me. 'You were caught by the toe tree. I think the forest likes you.' He flicks a caterpillar off his ear. 'It seems to have changed its mind.'

'On what?'

'To curse or bless you.'

The boy and Matias smile at each other.

'Right.' I feel out of it and embarrassed.

'Toe is sacred.' The boy looks down into his bowl. 'Shamans use it for healing. It's one of the five key plants. It either heals people or kills them.'

'Oh.'

He lifts a bowl off the workbench and comes over to me. 'Hungry?' He flicks brown hair out of his face. 'It's plantain and rice.' He has no shirt on and his shorts are dripping.

'Did you spit in it?' I've seen videos of jungle people chewing manioc in their mouths and spitting it back in the pot. It's the way they make mash.

He shakes his head and his eyes go smiley and something about him makes me trust him. Though I don't know why. It's like when you meet a dog and sense if it's going to let you stroke it or bite you.

'I'm Raul,' he says.

'Maya,' I say and take the bowl.

Maya

The food's nice – gentle and soft and sweet – but I still feel a bit sick. I haven't been knocked out twice in one day – or once any day – before.

'Do you know where Dad is?' I swallow a spoon and look at Matias. If Raul is a patting dog, Matias could be a biter. I don't know how to take him.

'Yeah.' He nudges a yellow spotted frog out the door with his foot. 'Kind of.'

'Kind of how?'

'Enough to know he wasn't kidnapped. He shot at me.'

I spit out the rice. 'He wouldn't do that.'

'He did and he missed.'

'Whoa!' Raul holds his hands up and looks at Matias. 'He shot at you?'

Matias shrugs.

'You mentioned trees. You never mentioned guns.' Raul folds his arms.

'You think I expected guns?' Matias stares him out.

Raul raises his eyebrows. 'Yeah, after what happened. Yeah, I reckon you should've expected guns.'

'After what happened?' I grip the bowl. No one answers. 'Dad doesn't have a gun.' I think about the shot in the night. I don't know who it came from, but it wasn't him.

'Well he did. He shot at me and left.' He scratches his ear and looks away, 'with a guy with a briefcase.'

'Why would he do that?' I pull a face.

'I don't know.'

'You don't know?' Raul yells. 'How can you not know? I thought you knew everything.'

'I know what he's *doing*. I just don't know *why*.' Matias waves his hands.

'I don't get it.' I rub my hand over my forehead. 'None of this makes sense.'

Matias looks at me. 'Your dad's a fool,' he says.

I look at his face and wish I'd hit him harder with the paddle. 'My dad's a scientist.'

'In the wrong hands everyone's a fool,' he says. In what hands? The hands of the guy with the briefcase?

I pick up the other boot and chuck it at him. He ducks but it catches his shoulder.

Matias stands up and runs his fingers through his hair. 'You two have the same enemy,' he says.

'Like how?' Raul shoots him a look.

'But I have the solution. Help me finish my boat and I'll take you downriver and we'll find out what you need to know.' He puts his bowl on the table and his hands on his hips. 'And stop the worst from happening.'

'I thought the worst already happened.' Raul's eyes narrow.

'Me too,' I say into my food.

'No.' Matias shakes his head. 'The worst is about to happen. If we don't stop Maya's father, everything will be worse.'

Raul

Maya looks so mad I think light beams are going to come out of her eyes and burn Matias alive.

'How?' She looks at her knees. '*How* will it be worse?'

'That's what we need you to find out.' Matias rubs his elbows. 'But not right now. It's late.'

He yawns and stares out the doorway. The breeze blows his hair. 'You need sleep. We all do.'

'I'm not tired,' she says and grips her spoon so tight her knuckles are white.

A flicker like a light mosquito flies out of Maya.

No one else seems to notice.

It looks at me and buzzes off.

Maya stares at Matias.

Matias stares at the night.

The rain stops.

And the silence feels like a visitor that comes in and sits with us. *Hey, I'm silence.*

We don't shake its hand. No one smiles at it.

Matias scratches his head. 'OK, OK, I'll tell you what I know,' he says. 'Out there, not in here.' He points at the door. 'Some words need space, you know.'

He offers Maya his shoulder to lean on. She puts her arm on it though her face says she doesn't want to touch him. Her leg says she has no choice. They shuffle out on to the veranda. I unhook a lantern from the roof and follow. Steven trots out too and we all sit together on the floor swatting away giant moths, breathing in the wet heat.

'OK,' Matias says and breathes out. 'Don't blame me if you can't take it.'

The darkness sits and listens.

Maya

'My name is Matias Fernandez,' he says and sits and leans his back against the hut. 'I've lived in the jungle *all* my life.' He looks over at Raul.

Raul pulls a face and puts two fingers up at him.

'And for as long as I have been alive I have loved trees. They suck things up, they spit things out, they breathe. They have soul.' Matias closes his eyes. 'My father used to teach me how to use them, how to treat them. Respect. He taught me how to respect the trees. And it was trees that killed my father.'

Raul tucks his hands under his arms. 'It wasn't the trees. It was the people.'

Matias shoots him a look. 'It was money.'

'It was the people after the money.'

The rain mist smokes out of the wood and the forest sighs. Two moths with pink eyes and long green tails land next to the lamp. Steven eats one.

Matias stares Raul out. Neither of them blinks. 'We should know better than to slaughter what is precious,' Matias says. 'But we don't. We don't learn. We care about money.'

'Dad doesn't care about money,' I tell them. It's true, he could be rich, but he isn't. He never takes on a job 'cos of what it pays.

'No, the way they've trapped him is different.' Matias frowns. 'I haven't worked it out yet.'

'Who's they?'

'JVF,' he says. 'Juan Carlos Vial Forestal.'

Raul

JVF. Even hearing the name makes me feel sick. Steven snuffles his nose under my knees.

Maya looks confused.

'They're a deforestation company,' I tell her.

Matias nods.

'They used to be little. Now they're not.'

'They cut down one thousand hectares of forest last year.' Matias points around us. 'It takes five years to grow a tree this thick . . .' He cups his hands into a circle. 'One hundred years this thick . . .' He spreads his arms like they're hugging the air.

'They can't do that.' Maya throws her arms up. 'Doesn't the government protect the forest? Aren't there laws?'

I scratch behind Steven's ears. 'Gangs cut the wood and ride it downriver to export. They have guns.' I look at Matias. 'No one argues. The government turns a blind eye or backs it.'

'They fake the exportation papers,' Matias says. 'They lie about where they're taking the wood from. They say they're taking it legally, but they don't. And no one checks.' Matias stares at Maya. 'Two years ago we joined the EIA.'

'You joined,' I say under my breath.

'The Environmental Investigation Agency.' Matias says. 'We work undercover.' He puffs out his cheeks. 'We have to. My uncle joined too. He moved downriver to Belen and started tracking shipments. The carrier's too big for Belen so it docks offshore and small boats ferry the wood from Iquitos. Loads of them. Small boats heaped so high that the ship sits heavy in the water, fat like a pig while the forest's left with holes and scars.'

'Why would people do that?' Maya screws up her eyes.

'For money – everyone's desperate for the money,' he says. 'They sell it on for millions.'

'JVF have a new project,' he says. 'Two thousand hectares. Here in Iquitos.'

My stomach fills with acid.

I try to catch Matias's eye, but he just looks at Maya. 'They fought off the small gangs and turned into an official "corporation". Now the government backs them, but last year there was a law passed protecting the trees, so even JVF can't do this without official approval.'

We look at Maya.

'My father isn't in the government.'

I look at Matias. 'They need scientific approval, right?'

'Right.' Matias nods.

'My father would never approve that.' Maya pulls her knees in tight.

'No?' Matias taps a finger on his foot. 'He will do at four o'clock next Thursday. Unless you stop him.'

'Why?' Maya flicks away a black and yellow spotted grasshopper.

'I don't know.' Matias shakes his head. 'You need to find your dad and find out.'

'Right.' Maya raises her eyebrows. 'Like he'll listen to me,' she whispers and folds her arms.

'You're the one that'll get her there.' Matias pokes my elbow.

'Where?' I ask like I don't know. My heart sinks.

'JVF offices. Iquitos.' He taps between my

eyebrows. 'You've got the heart for it. After—'

'Yeah. Yeah, I know,' I say. After what happened. He doesn't need to say it.

'Maya, you've got the fire for it.' He winks at me.

Maya looks at him sideways. 'What were you going to do if I didn't fall out of the tree? Kidnap me?'

Matias shrugs. 'Yeah, maybe. But the tree was kinda handy.'

'Thanks.' She rolls her eyes.

'Look, people have died. People get shot. Peope get burned alive. We do this for them. We do it because we have to.'

Matias puts a finger on the top of our heads.

'So are you in?'

Raul

Maya sleeps on the table. Matias gets his hammock and I have to sleep on the floor.

Sleep? No way I'm getting to sleep.

That's the problem with a one-room house. No place to talk about problems and everything's public. You want to talk about something, you go into the trees. I remember my parents doing it. Coming back with tight faces or smiles depending how it went.

I lie there and listen to their breath getting deeper. Slower. Hear them drifting off.

It's funny how you can feel someone's asleep, like they're disconnected. Or not.

I remember how I used to feel it with my brothers. Like their radio frequency stopped. It's like awake energy has a fizzle. We sense more than we know. The jungle's all about sense. You need to sense 'cos everything's so in-your-face you can't see.

The past tiptoes in and sits next to me and won't go away. A shadow like a monkey that sits and watches.

Since Alessa died it comes and I can't shake it. I never know when though. Sometimes it stares at me when I'm having fun. When I laugh. Like it's saying I shouldn't. Like it's saying I'm not sorry enough. It comes when I'm alone. That's the worst. That's when I run to Papi Rosales.

Maybe it's the past and maybe it's guilt. I know guilt though. Guilt's like a bag you carry that you can't put down. Like it's stuck to you and you can't shake it off. Sometimes it's lighter and you almost forget it's there. But it always is. Sometimes it's like rocks and makes you think you can't breathe.

Right now my chest feels heavy.

I creep my body up on to my feet, tiptoe out the door and jump off the veranda. Me and my house need to meet. There's too much unsaid between us.

The rain's stopped and has made clouds that are rising into the trees, lit by the moon.

I walk over slowly. Past the bit where our mamis used to hang out, the bit where we lit fires at night and took turns telling stories that used to scare the pants off me. And look at what used to be home.

My breath is shallow. My stomach's tight.

The light is grey and hazy.

It looks wrong seeing our place wrapped up in forest, like the vines are trying to cover up we ever existed. Or maybe they're just holding it steady for us. Hoping we'll come back one day.

I stand outside.

It's like a cowboy stand-off. Like the house is saying, 'You coming in or what?' Like neither of us wants to make the first move.

I hold my elbows though it's not cold. It's never cold here. It's the only place I feel warm.

I walk over to the steps. A bird screams out. I jump but keep going.

Our house looks like Matias's. Steps up the back with a veranda we used to jump off out the front. 'Cept the vines are so thick it's like the jungle's eating it. No way I can climb up without machete-ing it all down and cutting my way in.

'I'm sorry,' I say, though the words just hang about in the air like clouds. Meaning nothing.

'I am,' I say.

I put my hand on the wood. And it's like a vibe flows up my hand into my body.

I pull my hand away and run back to the house and curl up on the floor like I never went anywhere.

Maya

I blink away my dreams, full of running and trees, and rub my eyes in the light.

Raul is over on one side of the hut. Asleep. Matias is nowhere, but I hear him clunking about outside.

I realise I'm starving. A trumpeter bird flies into the hut and screeches at me. It's white fluffy back feathers and bendy legs flutter as its screeching sound goes up and down.

Noise is the thing I first noticed when we landed in Lima two weeks ago. It never stops.

Music pouring out of car windows, playing on street corners. Policemen's whistles and batons on plastic shields, car horns all through the night. And birds. Dipping up and down, looping songs of birds on the other side of the world.

You hear the birds in the city, but you don't see them there.

You do here.

The bird hops along the floor looking at me. Its

head cocked to one side. Steven runs in with a grub hanging out of his mouth and it flies away. He eats the grub and juice squirts out on to the scorch line the light-ball creature burned on the wood yesterday.

'That's gross,' I say. But he doesn't seem to care or notice. I climb down. And notice my ankle feels a bit better. Better enough to take my weight anyway. I trace the line on the floor and crawl outside. Steven follows and looks over my shoulder.

'What *was* that?' I whisper and point at the line.

Steven shrieks and runs off, and Matias climbs up with a cup of coca tea and puts it next to my head.

I cover the line with my hand. 'So what's next for the guardians of the forest?' I sip the tea. It tastes like leaf mould and bark but it's hot.

Matias turns from looking out at the forest. 'Breakfast,' he says but doesn't smile. 'Then we finish the canoe.'

Raul

I wake up to the hum of the jungle. My head busy with questions my dreams threw up. I go out and find Matias and Maya on the deck. Matias grins, then jumps over the edge and disappears. He comes back with pitahaya fruit and starts throwing them to us. We have to catch them without dropping or busting our hands. Pitahaya are like fruit hand grenades. Yellow and bobbly. He throws one at Maya's head.

She catches it. 'Ow.'

'If you pull your shirt over your hands it doesn't hurt as much,' I say and catch three.

We sit and scoop out the sweet watery insides from the knobbly yellow skin with spoons.

Maya looks down at the mass of white with black specks. 'Do you eat the pips?'

'Yup,' I nod and slice open two more. I've got used to hot sweet quinoa milk and quinoa porridge in the town. Quinoa everything. No quinoa in the jungle.

The jungle fruits up bananas and roots and grubs and fish.

We feast on stripped-back fresh bananas, then take turns to wash the night sweat off in Matias's shower. It's a home-made rain catcher with water butt. The sun heats the water. The butt catches the rain. A metal pipe sprinkles it over your head. It has no roof. When it rains you just stand in the cubicle and take the water fresh from the sky.

Me and Matias stand under the veranda while Maya takes hers.

'How do we even know we can we trust her?' I whisper. If her dad's helping JVF, who knows what she really thinks? It's risky.

Matias stamps his feet at an approaching boa. The snake sniffs the air with its tongue, turns its head and slithers away. 'The forest likes her. I trust the forest,' he says, and goes into the woods to get plants to heal Maya's ankle.

We sit together on the veranda. It feels embarrassing. I don't know anything about Maya except her dad is helping the people I hate most in the world.

It makes her quite difficult to like.

Maya's hair's still wet from the shower and drips on the wood. The water evaporates.

'We came here for my dad's research,' she tells me, like she's answering the questions I want to ask but don't. 'Well, I thought we did. He's a scientist.' Her hair hangs over her face and she crosses her arms. I see a big blue bruise on her elbow. 'He studies light.'

We look up at the light. Thick and green and coming down in tunnels where the leaves part and sway in the wind.

She doesn't look at me.

'Where's your mum?'

'She disappeared when I was three. Don't ask.'

I don't.

I wonder how it feels to be that alone. Yeah, we moved and at first I didn't know anyone, but I always had my parents and my brothers. Even though they're so annoying sometimes I sit on their heads. Dad would walk in and say, 'What's going on here?' and I would say, 'I'm sitting on their heads.' They'd laugh under my butt and he'd scratch his and walk out.

'Where's yours?' she says.

'My mami?'

She nods.

'Back home.'

'You live near here?'

'Not any more.' I shake my head. I don't say that in my heart I've always lived here. In my heart I've never left.

'My dad's usually nice,' she says and grips her hand into fists. 'Kind of. Well, he was. He is. I'm sure he is. He's just . . .'

'What?'

'Got lost,' she says and scrapes bits of wood up with her fingernails. 'I didn't know about any of this.'

She sets her eyebrows and looks like she's trying not to cry. If it was me I'd want to hit something. If it was me I'd hate him. Emotions are complicated.

'I'm not sad, I'm angry, by the way,' she says and bunches up her toes. 'Being angry makes me want to cry.'

I won't know what to do if she cries. If she was my sister I'd hug her. But she isn't my sister. 'Look! A squirrel monkey!' I say and point into a tree.

It jumps off a branch and throws a stick at us.

'That means it likes you,' I say.

She smiles.

The trees ripple with its brothers and sisters. Hundreds of yellow-grey monkeys with pink fluffy ears and big eyes. They screech and swing their way away.

I want to ask her about her, about why she glows. I guess she doesn't know though, if she doesn't know she does it. How can you be magic and not know?

'What's that?' I point at a scorch line that leads into the house.

'Nothing.' She turns away and bum-shuffles inside. 'You like chocolate?' she yells.

'Sure, who doesn't?' I yell back, and she crawls out with a bright orange packet. Sugar's my thing. White chocolate, cola, *alfajores*; butter cookies sandwiched with caramel.

'Peace offering.' She holds up the very melted squishy bar. 'But I think all the pieces might have melted,' she says, and passes over chocolate heaven.

Maya

Peace offering. How bad is that line? I groan inside. He must hate me. My dad's helping the people who strip and kill the forest. I'd hate me.

Raul doesn't groan. He grins and takes the bar. 'Peace offering for what?' He throws a banana to a monkey looking down on us, with thick springy hair like it's wrapped in woolly foam. It catches it with a foot and swings away into the canopy. 'It isn't your fault.'

I shrug. At least chocolate's a start.

He holds the bar. It droops. 'I think snapping it in half would be overly optimistic.'

Raul peels the wrapper open so it doesn't spill and eats it.

I look away and wait for my half.

Two blue macaws fly over our heads.

He passes the bar over and I eat the leftover hot salty chocolate deliciousness. It tastes of home. My stomach churns with pleasure. I eat it slowly and let the sugar sting my tongue. I leave a centimetre in the middle. 'Do you mind spit?'

'Not much.'

'Then you can have the middle,' I say and pass it back.

'Thanks,' he says. 'I think.'

'How come you two speak so much English,' I say and watch our legs swing over the edge of the veranda. I look at his hairy brown ones. Mine're like milk bottles with red bites.

'My mum taught me,' he says and a sadness creeps over his face. Like I get to see inside him for a second. 'She taught the kids in our village. She said it'd come in useful. If we want to earn money.'

'Do you?'

'Everyone wants money.' He wipes the chocolate off his nose. 'Kind of.'

I look at his clothes and his pack with next to nothing in it. He doesn't really look like someone who wants money. Who's into stuff. The way he sits here in the jungle. Like he belongs. Like having nothing makes him happy.

'All the Spanish I know is, "Cheese" and "thank you". Pretty much.'

He smiles. 'Shouldn't it be "please" and "thank you"?'

I smile back.

Steven jumps up on to the decking and makes the chocolate wrapper into a hat. I feel a warm happy sugar glow come up from my stomach.

And the light ball pops out from behind Raul and drifts over to me.

Raul

A round ball of heat, like a pom-pom with eyes, scoots over the floor and hides behind Maya.

'What's that?'

'Nothing.'

I lean over to see.

She leans back to hide it.

'Ow.' She flinches.

We both smell smoke. 'I think your shirt's on fire.'

She wafts it away. 'I think your fly's undone.'

I look down.

Matias jumps up on to the veranda, 'What's cooking?'

'Nothing.' We freeze.

I put the fire in Maya's shirt out and the smoke disappears. So does the creature. I look behind Maya at a tennis-ball-shaped hole in the floor.

She raises her eyebrows at me and shrugs, and mouths, *I have no idea*, as our eyes meet.

I cock my head and shake it, like, *Let's not tell Matias*. It's nice to have our own secrets.

I turn to Matias. 'Did you get the plants?'

'Yeah,' he says and stares at us. 'You OK?'

'Sure.' Maya nods.

'Yep.' I kick the lantern from last night over the hole.

Stephen chatters and runs off with the wrapper into the cupboard, and we go inside to watch Matias make the plants into a healing paste.

Matias makes the paste and paints it on Maya's ankle and wraps it up.

'Now we work on the canoe,' Matias says, and passes her the paddle to use as a crutch to hold herself up. She hobbles down the steps and round to the front of the house.

'It's all in the wood.' Matias strokes the trunk he's carved out. He's done a good job. It's beautiful. I don't tell him though. His head's big enough. 'This'll last for twenty years,' he says and hands us two pots of dark green waterproofing and brushes made of wood and hair bristles. He squats to sand the final curve.

'Don't overlap it too much or spread it so thick

120

it goes clumpy.' He frowns and picks a bit off I've just done.

'Don't you trust us?' Maya dabs at the wood.

'Matias doesn't trust anyone but the trees.' I squat and paint a long stroke under the bow.

'Not just trust, respect.' Matias goes back to sanding. 'I don't trust the trees, I respect them.'

Me and Maya work on waterproofing. It takes ages 'cos Matias checks on us every five seconds, flicking between us and the cookout. Smells of roasting meat drift over. It smells so good it makes me dribble. Wood smoke from the fire soaks into our hair and clothes.

We stop for lunch. The meat is crispy and delicious. Skin crackled, inside so juicy it runs down my arms. I rip mouthfuls off the bone with spoons of rice. My stomach growls with pleasure. I try not to think about Narizo my pet capybara.

It's dark when we finish. We rub our eyes. Everything aches from squatting.

Matias lights the kerosene lamps and brings one down and holds it over the canoe.

We squint as the light floods over us.

Matias strokes the top and squats to check the shape of the canoe. 'When JVF came to our village it

121

was like vultures walked in.' He looks at Maya. 'They had the smell of death about them. Heavy. Like dark clouds with AK47s.'

We freeze. And rise. Matias's story pulls us up.

'Kids screamed and ran away, or hid behind their mothers, who took them in the house and peered out through the windows. It was the first time most of us had seen guns. Or outsiders. They wanted to speak to my father.'

I see it when he tells it. Try to block it out but I can't.

'When he came it turned out what they really wanted was for us to work for them for shiny junk they pulled out of their bags and tried to impress us with, like we were birds collecting flowers for their nest. Like we could be won over that easy.

'When it didn't work they tried money.

'Dad said, "Why do we need money when we live with such riches," and pointed round us, and they peppered the canopy with bullets and everything screeched and flew and ran.

'They got workers in from outside instead.' Matias moves his hands like a bird flying in. 'Ferried them in on motorised boats with chainsaws that ripped into the

122

wood and whined. Wheels of metal teeth screaming like we could hear the trees crying as they fell.'

I wonder what they remember of it. I wonder what memories of this are stored in the trees, why didn't the spirits come?

'We tried to keep on living amongst it. Nothing we could do. Till it happened.'

Matias walks round the edges of the canoe, stroking the top of the wood. He looks right at me. I look away. Guilt sits in my belly like gold bars.

'My father was crushed by *aguano, caoba*.' He runs his fingers over the wood. 'Mahogany,' he says. 'Tons and tons of mahogany.'

I look at Maya. 'Log slide.'

She nods.

'My father paid for their greed. My father was a sacrifice for the pain of the trees. A life for a life. Taken to Pachamama. Straight. Crushed so far into the mud they never found his body.'

We stand there for a minute. Like the silence can soak the pain up.

I tell the end. This is my story too. 'JVF overcut and overpiled the wood.' I make my hands into fists. 'It rained and the wood slid. The workers

123

didn't know what they were doing. Not properly. These guys were cheap and they didn't care. Everyone in the village was freaked out. It was a sign and everyone moved. We had to go.'

'Had to?' Matias cocks his head.

'Yeah.' I fold my arms. 'Had to.' This row's gone on since we went. I thought he was over it. If he stayed, everyone should've stayed. Yeah right. Everyone was terrified.

'Everything happens for a reason, right?' Matias says and beckons us over to the house and we follow. 'I like to think his soul's recycled.' He touches the tips of a young tree growing next to the upright of the balcony. 'I planted this when he went.'

The soil round Matias's papi's plant is so neatly tended and weeded, nothing else could grow there.

I put my hand on his shoulder.

'I'm sorry,' Maya says.

'Me too.' Matias strokes a leaf.

We stand there looking at the tree.

In the pool of light, insects flood around us. Shadows swoop on to the lamp.

From behind something cracks. My belly jumps. 'What's that?'

'What?' Maya turns and out of the dark reaches an arm. An arm that turns into a man.

She screams.

Matias yells.

I back off back to the house and fall.

And a woman steps out into the light and gets Maya in a headlock.

Maya

I feel Rosa's arms round my throat and try to pull free.

Matias spins and grabs Charles. I see his face in the light. Frog eyes. I twist round and see hers behind me. Same as I first saw round the lodge fire.

She pulls backwards and I bite her and run to the canoe. Raul's already there and grabs the other paddle out and whirls it round his head.

I pick my paddle-crutch up and smack it into Rosa's face when she comes for me and push the handle into her stomach.

Charles punches Matias who falls over the back of the canoe. I hear it crack as he lands.

Rosa's pulling herself up. Raul is taking on Charles and dancing out of his way.

'Leave the boy, get the girl,' he yells, and Rosa runs at me. I dodge and she slips in the mud.

Charles wraps both his arms round my waist.

I scream and kick backwards with my good leg,

but he doesn't let go.

Out of the trees screams Steven, who drops on to Charles's head. His little fists pummelling his eyes. 'Eeeeeeeeeeeee.' He lets go.

Matias stands and grabs Rosa, twists her arm up her back.

'Let's go.' Raul takes my hand.

'What about the canoe?'

'We can't run with a canoe.'

'We can't leave without it.'

Charles detaches Steven like a hat.

Rosa elbows Matias in the stomach and Matias turns and snuffs the lamp out so everyone is left in darkness. 'Go!' he yells.

And me and Raul hobble-run into the jungle. Hidden. Till the torches come.

I pull him off the trail and we squat in the mud. The pain's so bad I think I'm going to be sick. 'I can't run any more,' I whisper.

Torch beams cut through the trees and bounce off pairs of eyes. We duck out of the way of the light arms reaching though everything to snatch us.

'Shut your eyes,' I say.

Too late.

Their torches flash over our heads and the light catches Raul.

'Over here!' Rosa yells and runs, knees up, into the green and thorns like she's going for a medal.

I think of the trees. I think of Matias's dad.

And I am angry. I stand.

Raul gets up and pulls me. 'Run!'

I ball my hands into fists. The wind blows my hair. I don't run.

I stay.

Rosa dives for my ankles.

And out of the ground come balls of light, multiplying and rising like fireflies. Like rain the wrong way up. Rosa burns her arm on one and pulls back. The balls glow yellow in the dark, making a line between us. A hum rises up from them as they rise. They start to shake and eyes pop on to their vibrating burning bodies.

I grip my fists.

The balls squeeze and shudder and explode into a line of fire.

Raul

The fire spreads like a snake that separates the ground between us like an earthquake, and roars up into the sky in a tower of flames. It makes a wall between us and them, reaching from one side of the trail to the other, higher than their heads.

The man and woman shrink back and put their forearms in front of their faces. The light twists itself through the woods. A monkey screeches across the path.

The jungle shimmers. But the trees don't burn. Nothing does.

The man and woman charge at the wall, but scream and pull back. The fire holds them. Whichever way they turn. Whichever way they try to run.

We stand there watching. The fire doesn't come forward. Or back. It just dances.

Up and up.

'You know the way to the jetty?' Maya says.

I nod. 'Yeah. I think so.'

'What about Matias?'

'He told us to go.' I wipe the sweat off my face. 'If he wants to hide he'll hide so no one ever finds him. If he wants to come he'll find us.'

Maya tries to walk on her ankle and hops and squeaks.

I put her arm round my neck and my arm round her waist and feel awkward. 'OK?'

'OK.' She nods and looks awkward too.

'OK.' I twist away from the flames. Maya doesn't and we nearly fall over.

'Sorry.' She twists back and we use our arms to rebalance and blink away the brightness and head off into the dark. Hobbling like kids in a three-legged race. We don't look back.

Down the trail. Through the mud. Down the river steps and into a canoe.

A motorised canoe.

Waiting at the bottom.

Maya

I lift myself in.

'Whose boat is this?' Raul hops into the back.

'Theirs,' I say. I remember it from the jetty.

Raul smiles and pulls the engine chord and out of the undergrowth comes a screech and an 'eeeeee' that knocks me into a seat.

'We can't take Steven!' Raul yells. The boat races down the river in the dark.

'What d'you want me to do. Chuck him back?' Steven wraps his arms round my chest and closes his eyes. 'We can't not take him.' The air blasts over my face and mixes with the sweat.

A boat sails up towards us, lights on its outside.

Voices inside.

It keeps coming.

'Watch out!' I yell and put a hand over Steven's head.

Raul yells something in Spanish and we twist off round the side of it at the last second. The family cruise past and yell and wave their arms at us.

We buzz down the river. Branches overhanging on each side. Water bouncing over rocks in the middle. We stick to the edge. 'Aren't there any lights on this?' I search my fingers over the wood.

Raul scratches his neck and looks around and the boat veers.

'Watch the tree!'

He veers back on track and clicks a switch. The lights glow in lines up the sides and out the front. An anaconda's eyes glint in the light and it slides off the tree into the water. Steven hides under my knees.

I pull my boots off and hold my ankle like a broken bird.

'How did you do the fire?' Raul shouts above the engine. 'It was amazing.'

'I didn't.' I fold my arms and lean my head against the side of the boat and feel the hole in the back of my T-shirt where the light creature burnt it on the veranda. 'I didn't do anything. It wasn't me.'

Raul

I drive straight by the harbour at Iquitos.

'Shouldn't we be stopping?' Maya points at the jetty as we drift by.

'We need to keep you hidden.' I look back at her. She looks like a moon. A very thoughtful moon. 'You're kind of distinctive. If the canoe was meant to be coming back here, they might have people waiting for you, right?'

'Right,' she says and starts searching under the seats. Steven runs back and forth chattering. I think it's his first trip in a canoe.

'What are you looking for?'

'We have no clothes, food, water or money,' she says. 'So pretty much any of that.'

I switch the lights off and we pull into a bay I used to come to with Dad. We used to come fishing for yellow piranhas, and he taught me how to cook seafood soup with hot pepper. It was our place.

I step into the river and pull the canoe half on to

133

the bank. Half hidden from the water by a fallen trunk. You can't get here on land.

I hop back in and check my legs for leeches. They're clean, which is great as I don't fancy lighting a fire to get them off.

'Bingo,' Maya says and lifts two rucksacks out of the lifebelt storage compartment. She pulls them open.

We look through the rucksacks in the moonlight.

Rain poncho. Anti-mosquito spray. Jungle shirt. Two plastic passes.

Maya shines the torch from their pack on the passes. I hold them up and squint. The faces from the jungle look back at us

Maya tilts them so the light bounces off. 'Rosa Chavez and Charles Hinterguard.' She points to the logo at the bottom. 'JVF. Matias was right,' she says. 'You think he's OK?' The boat bobs and the water laps against the sides.

'Matias is a panther. When he wants to he just disappears.'

Maya reads the back: 'Plaza Napo 258.' We stare at the address. 'I guess that's where we go tomorrow, right?'

'Right,' I say, but my gut says, *NO WAY*.

Companies guard their offices with guns here. Even the banks do it. Guys in suits stand outside in shades with truncheons, cuffs and rifles. So big you see them from far away. So big no one messes.

Maya finds a wallet and flips it open. There's no cash. Just a photo of Rosa with her arms round two kids. Hugging them in tight. We stare at them. They grin back at us.

'You think she's doing this to make money for them?'

'I guess.' Maya shoves the photo back in the bag.

The thought makes me feel a bit sick. I don't want things to be complicated. I touch Aiko's parcel in my pocket. Life's easier when there's good guys and bad guys, right?

'We'll have to spend the night in here,' I say.

'Sure.' Maya shines the torch on the bank and we lay branches and leaves that I slice down from the trees with my knife over the boat.

She pulls back when she sees the size of the blade. 'You keep that in your shorts?'

'Yeah,' I say and hit Steven with a leaf 'cos he keeps chucking the roof in the river.

The moon looks down at us.

'Now we sleep, right?' she says.

'Right,' I say, and we climb back into the boat, with the wood digging into our butts, and try to get comfortable under the banana leaves. It's like trying to sleep on a piano.

Around us the river is alive with frogs chirping.

The boat rocks gently like something nudged it. Something BIG.

Maya sits up. 'Do caiman eat people?'

'Not really.' I stick a rucksack under my head. 'Anacondas do. But you have to be in the water to get got by one.' A dragonfly lands on my arm and I brush it off. 'The worst is candiru fish. If you pee in the water they swim up it and into your ...' I wiggle my finger. 'You know?'

'Yeah, I know. Can't you just pull it out?'

'No. It has barbs and gets stuck. They have to put a tube in so you wee into a plastic bag.'

'And it just lives in there?'

'Yeah.'

'Forever?'

'Uh-huh. They call it the vampire fish.'

'It must be pretty teeny,' she says and I laugh. 'I heard

there's a frog that if you lick it, it's hallucinogenic.'

'Yeah, there's lots of those. And don't go in the river when you've got your period.' I make my hand into a mouth. 'The piranhas will smell you out.'

'Right. I hadn't even been thinking about that. I hope I don't get mine before I get home.'

I try to imagine her home. How it must feel to be a million miles away.

We lie there in silence for a bit.

'I don't get where the light balls came from or why they started the fire,' Maya mumbles.

'They kinda came from you,' I say.

'They didn't.'

'OK.'

Neither of us says anything. Steven snores.

'You don't think it's weird?' she says.

'No.'

I don't tell her she glows when she's knocked out. Which is pretty weird. Pretty brilliant weird.

I think about Papi Rosales. *Magic happens,* he says. *Magic is all around us.*

I think about the firewall.

The fire was Maya.

It was.

The light balls came 'cos she called them.
She just doesn't know it.
Yet.

Raul

We buzz upriver. Back to Iquitos. Bellies full of berries we found this morning, and nerves.

I switch the engine off to kill the noise and drift into a bay before the harbour. No way we're going there in daylight if we can't go at night. We'll take the back way in.

I hop out and tie the boat up, and Maya takes the tags out and rereads the address. 'Plaza Napo 258. You know where that is?'

'Kind of.' I don't tell her about the guards and their guns. I guess she'll see that for herself soon enough. I wish Matias had told us more of the plan.

Maya steps out of the boat and I cut a trail, avoiding any spiders that fall. BUMF, one lands by my feet in a ball like a fist, then spreads its legs and scarpers. I scram and Maya laughs. I look at her and she stops.

We step out of the trees and look back at the harbour. Rusty double-decker river cruisers bob by a jetty that runs up into town to tin shacks and houses with reed roofs and yellow crumbling walls.

It's busy in the morning. People are hanging out and selling stuff. One guy with a rack of sunglasses, one guy with a load of Ekeko dolls; good-luck charms you stuff with cash and sweets. You can only give them to someone else. Buying good luck for yourself isn't allowed. I wish we had one.

I stare at Maya. She's like a piece of Lego in a bird's nest. Different. 'Everyone's going to see you here. You need a disguise.'

She pulls my hat off my head and shoves her hair under. 'Hey,' I yell.

'It works,' she whispers and pulls the brim down.

I guess it does. No one else round here has hair like fire.

We walk up the footbridge into town. I carry Steven who wriggles – it's like walking through a sea of sharks with a piece of steak. You never really notice how you blend in till you don't. Heads turn and stare at us. Two street dogs come and sniff our legs. Maya tries to pet one and I kick them away. 'Don't.'

'They're just dogs.' She stands up and the hat falls

off and her hair falls out.

'No one pets wild dogs. People'll notice,' I say. And I notice the shadow of a guy behind us walking two paces back. Always two paces back.

I slow up.

He slows.

And Maya pushes me behind the fish shack and gets out my knife.

Maya

Raul looks round the corner at the building I've been watching too. The one the follower's hiding behind.

We look at each other.

'You seen him?' I whisper.

He nods.

'You think we should cut my hair off?' I hold up the knife.

'If someone's seen you, they've seen you.' I take the knife back. 'I don't think losing your hair'll make any difference.'

'Who is he?'

'I have no idea.'

'You think we can lose him?'

'Maybe.'

'You need to give me your shirt,' I say. 'We need to swap. Then he might think you're me.'

'Is that a good thing?' He stares at me. At my jungle-explorer beige.

'Mine's not girly. It's just smart. Way too smart.

No one here dresses like this. If he tries to grab you I can run.'

'What about me?' Raul frowns.

'You can run fast. You can run faster.'

'You can make the fireballs.'

I kick his shin. 'No, I can't.'

We sneak round the corner and hide behind some bins in the woods, next to the riverbank. Steven sniffs around for food.

We crouch either side of a bin and stick our arms out and swap on three. Like rock, paper, scissors. One, two, three. Change.

I pull it over my head and officially smell like Raul.

It's weird.

'You wear name labels?' He laughs and pulls out the label.

I hate them. It makes me feel like I'm five. 'My Dad likes labels,' I say and go red. Last summer he got a plastic sticker machine and stuck labels all over everything in the house.

DRAWER

KNIVES

FORKS

I made one that said DAD and stuck it on his head and then he stopped. I think he got the message.

We stand up. Raul looks weird.

'Your name's Anderson, right?' We dust off our shorts.

'Yeah, so?'

'What's your dad's name?'

'Handi.'

He looks at me like I'm a ghost. 'We're not going to JVF,' he says. 'We're going to the El Dorado Hotel, Plaza de Aramas.'

'Why?'

'It's where your dad is.'

The shadow guy leans round the corner.

I grab Raul's hand and run.

Raul

We run before we even see his eyes. Down the riverbank, through the water and up the other side.

H. Anderson

It's the name on the parcel I held in the back of the DHL van, the one Omar had to deliver. Maybe we don't need an Ekeko doll. Maybe the gods just like us.

Maya hobble-runs and yells as we slide in the mud. Steven screeches alongside.

Her boot goes in my face.

We speed out of the reed-roof houses, though the crumbling streets, into the slick concrete slabs of the city. Maya is limping, we're both sweating. Steven keeps looking round, like, 'Where'd all the trees go?'

We slink round the back of the slick white walls of the El Dorado Hotel and squat next to a dumpster. We put our backs against the plastic, breathing hard.

The shadow walks round the edge of the building. The bins stink in the heat. We don't move.

Maya points round the side of the dumpster, near the door.

The guy's feet crunch in the dust.

We scuttle round the side like land crabs and swing into the hotel, past a guy with a cigarette on his way out. He nearly burns my shoulder.

'Sorry,' we say and blink our eyes in the corridor dark and carry Steven into the toilet.

And lock the door.

Maya

I stick my head under the cold tap. Steven swipes the water with a paw. I come up for air and we swap over. Raul sticks his head in then switches the tap off and we lean against the sinks and breathe.

'My dad doesn't stay in hotels,' I say.

'Well, he was here on Friday.'

I put my hand over my mouth. 'This place stinks.'

'I know.' Raul covers his nose. 'I had to deliver a parcel. In a truck. And a plane. Your dad's name was on the parcel.'

I squint at the strip light and switch it off. I feel calmer in the dark. Dark feels safe. We stand there and blink our eyes to get used to the half-light pouring in under the door like someone that's been steamrollered.

'My dad would *never* stay here.' He wouldn't. He's never stayed in a big hotel in his life. His principles used to annoy everyone, especially me.

'Well, he is.' Raul nods. 'Get over it.'

Steven comes out from under the toilet and jumps into the sink.

I twist my finger in my elbow and try not to breathe. 'If he's there, he won't let me in. He thinks I've gone home anyway.'

'He'll recognise your voice.'

'He won't tell me what's happening.' The idea of seeing Dad when he's involved in all this suddenly makes me feel sick. 'If I ask at the hotel desk they might have someone waiting, watching out.' I rub the back of my neck.

'JVF?'

I nod. I wish I knew what to do. I wish Matias had told us the plan. 'You'll have to pretend to be room service.' I look round at the cubicle. 'I actually do need a wee. Could you turn round please.'

Raul clutches Steven by the sink. 'What's the difference between roast beef and pea soup?' I say loud enough to distract from the noise.

'Anyone can roast beef,' I yell.

And BOOM.

Someone bangs on the door.

Raul

Maya opens the door and pushes it back on to the person's head as they start to come in. He swears and grabs his face and we run out into the kitchen.

Everyone's so busy nobody notices.

Maya hides Steven and squats by a cupboard.

I walk out of the kitchen carrying a bowl of *aguadito de pollo*. Chicken soup.

Fast.

In the corridor Maya and Steven scuttle after me, and the air-conditioning hits us like an iceberg. I walk into the lobby while they wait round the corner next to the lifts. Steven keeps pressing the buttons so they light up. Then trying to eat them.

'Mr Anderson ordered this. I forgot the room number,' I say.

The receptionist looks at me closely.

I look at the single line of grey hair streaking up her head. She looks at me over the top of her glasses and leans back in her chair. The phone rings. She talks.

I point at the soup. 'It's going cold,' I say, and make a face.

She looks behind and mouths the number.

'Doscientos tres.'

Two hundred and three.

And Steven bursts in round the corner.

Maya

Steven escapes. He runs. I run after Steven. Raul spills the soup and Steven starts licking it up off the floor. The woman behind the desk screams and I scoop him under my arm and put him out the front door. 'Wait there!' I say, and he gives me big eyes.

The receptionist stands and yells at me. 'Sorry!' I yell back and run out.

Raul catches me in the corridor. 'Two zero three,' he says and I look at the board of keys on the wall.

Room 203.

I see the key. Top row behind the receptionist who sits back down.

I also clock a CCTV camera trained on the desk. And one on the lifts. I wonder if they enjoyed the Steven and me show.

'The keys are too high. Plus they've got CCTV,' I say.

'So.'

'So it's impossible.'

Raul wipes soup off his shirt. He looks at the key rack. He looks back at me. 'You know in my country there are two thousand nine hundred and thirty-seven species of birds and animals. Sixteen per cent of them don't exist anywhere else in the world. Thirty-one per cent of the plants don't exist anywhere else either. If they cut down those trees they will die. Hundreds of birds and monkeys and baby monkeys will die.'

'All right, all right!' I put my hands over my ears. 'I can't bear it.' I scream in frustration and a ball of yellow pops out of the staircase and looks at us, then hovers over into reception.

The receptionist's eyes bulge.

I look on in horror as it spreads itself against the wall by the lifts and sets the wallpaper on fire.

The fire alarms go off.

Raul

The receptionist runs over with an extinguisher.

Fire starts licking up the wallpaper.

'You can't do that!' Maya tells the fireball off as it drifts back to us. 'You can't just go round doing things like that!' she shouts at it and it shrinks to the size of a pea and disappears.

She eyeballs me. 'You did that deliberately. You made me mad on purpose.'

'It was an experiment,' I smile.

We stare at the fire. The fuss everyone's making about it. It pulls everyone in.

Steven keeps leaping at the window from outside, like a kangaroo on mountain dew. I try not to laugh.

Maya runs in and stands on the receptionist's chair and snatches the key. We put our hands over our ears and run for the staircase. Everybody else is running down.

We run up.

We reach the floor and speed walk along the corridor.

I see the numbers. 213, 209, 205 . . .

We swing through a double door. And stand outside two zero three as the door at the other end of the corridor slams shut. And freeze.

Maya

The door at the other end slams shut and I see a blur that I'm sure is my dad run through it. It's like we're slipping into different dimensions.

We freeze.

'You going in or what?' Raul nudges me.

'I want to know if he's in first.' I knock.

No one answers.

I slide the key in and open the door.

Inside, the room's like a photo with the person missing. Just all background.

The door clicks shut and the noise of the fire alarm dims.

The wardrobe's open. I see Dad's shirts hanging there.

His watch is on the bedside table. His bed is unmade. A pencil and notepad covered in doodles lie on the bench, and a big brown briefcase sits on the bed.

Raul looks in the bathroom then comes out and checks through the drawers.

'What are you looking for?'

'Food.' He opens the fridge and chucks me a bottle of water.

It's so weird being in here with Dad's smell. And no Dad.

Raul takes all the food he can find out of the fridge and the fruit bowl and stuffs it into the rucksack. He holds up two bottles of yellow cola and grins. He kisses one and takes a drink.

I look at the briefcase and open it.

Raul

Maya looks different in here, like she's seen a ghost.
I guess she has.

It's weird being in someone's room when they're
not in it. Like they've just walked out of their life.
Like he's just walked out of hers.

I think about the way I left my dad. He'll be on
his way home right now. To face Mum. And tell her
about me. She'll kill him. I blink my eyes hard and
look in the drawers.

I don't really know what I'm looking for till I find
Maya's dad's wallet. It's just lying there.

Stealing is not what I do. Stealing is not what I've
ever done. Bad stuff comes back at you. That's the
way life works.

But we're alone. With no one. And nothing.

When I left my rucksack at Matias's I lost my
money too. We need money, right?

I open the wallet and shove the cash in the

157

rucksack and pile food on top fast so Maya doesn't notice. I put the wallet back in the drawer.

She opens the briefcase that's lying on the bed. I lean over her shoulder to see what's in it but don't get to because the door bursts open and someone grabs Maya over their shoulder and runs off down the corridor.

Maya

When he lifts me up I don't waste time screaming. I ball my fists and summon up all my fire and let it out. A fireball bounces out of the air and up to the roof, blazing a trail as it skims the walls. It's out of control. A raw spirit that burns him on the elbow, the knee. Jabbing in and out. The man holds me high in the air and yells, 'No burning, no burning!' He doesn't let go.

It isn't Charles. It's someone else.

I think someone might notice. Someone might help. But in the chaos of the fire alarm no one's here and no one does.

I see Raul running down the corridor after us, clinging on to both rucksacks, Dad's door left open.

The fireball weaves up and around us like a sparkler. The man runs down the stairs and out into the heat, yelling stuff I don't know in Spanish, and tips me into the back of a three-wheeler mototaxi.

'Stay!' He points at me like a dog and turns to yell

something at Raul. The ball loses control of itself in the wind.

Steven comes screaming across the car park and throws himself in through the open window. The fireball jumps into the back with us. I hold Steven close and he snuffles his nose into my hand and the ball bursts like a bubble and disappears.

Raul says something in Spanish and jumps in with the bags and the guy starts the engine, which sounds like a can of flies in a sardine tin.

Raul

We bump off down the street, held in by walls as thin as plastic lunch boxes and big empty gaps where windows should be.

'We should jump.' Maya gets up clutching Steven and puts one foot on the window edge.

I pull her back.

The mototaxi swerves round a corner and our heads hit the seat in front. Hot air blows in as we pull ourselves back up on to the seat, and blast past three guys leaning against a green garage and rusty pickups with families sharing jugs of juice in the back.

'It's OK,' I say, and we skid across the seat round another corner.

'Yeah, right.' Maya stops herself from falling out the window with her elbow.

I yell, 'Watch the road, watch the road!' We miss two women with flowers on their backs and a whole family on a red motorbike.

161

'No really, it's OK,' I tell her, and we screech to a halt. We're in Belen, on the edge of the town at the start of the water, the floating town in the city. The engine stops.

'Maya, meet Carlos,' I say. 'Uncle of Matias.'

Maya

What? 'You could've said.' I look at Raul.

'I tried to say.'

'When?'

Uncle Carlos opens the door as we stare at each other.

'Carlos,' he says.

'Maya,' I say and shake his hand.

I watch Raul and Carlos hug and say stuff I don't understand.

'And this is Steven,' I say. The agouti is now clinging to me like a baby lemur.

We get out and follow him on to a jetty with a boat like a canoe made of reeds wrapped round plastic bottles and get it in.

'Sorry,' Raul says and scratches his ear.

Carlos smiles and winks at me.

'He could've just said,' I whisper. 'He didn't need to grab me.'

'Everyone knows who he is here. They know he works for the EIA.'

I picture all the little boats floating out of here stacked. Ferrying out the forest like worker ants. 'He isn't that popular, right?'

'He's had death threats. He didn't want to draw attention to us in town.' Raul scratches his neck. 'He says we were always meant to meet him. Matias just never told us. Yet.'

I think of the fire in the forest. Of Matias on the other side of it.

I guess the time for telling us got cut short.

We slide down the river and look out at the families who live in the wooden reed-roof shacks raised out of the water on stilts. Two kids play swinging off a metal bar that sticks out of the water like a goalpost with no net and one of them falls off.

They both shriek-laugh and the other one drops in too.

It feels like floating past a sea of eyes. Everyone stares at us.

Carlos stands on the back and pushes us along with a pole paddle. The boat glides and the sunlight dances everywhere. We pass two women in felt skirts, with purple woollen tights and pom-poms in their hair descaling fish with knives.

CLICK. I take their photo with my brain.

Raul dips his fingers in the water.

A family boat goes past laughing. Two of the boys start fighting about whose frog is the biggest and the dad chucks them both in the water.

SPLASH.

I look at the reflection of my face wobbling in the ripples.

We pull up to a house that's standing proud out of the water, long and thin with squares cut out for windows and a ladder up. Carlos says something to Raul and pulls the canoe in against wooden floating boards that connect the houses together like a pavement.

'He says we'll be safe here while we wait for instructions,' Raul says.

We step out and climb up the ladder into the house where we meet two women with long black hair plaited down their backs. They smile at us and give us steaming-hot bowls of quinoa soup.

We sit down at the table and the whole room rises from cushions spread across the floor, and we are surrounded by intrigue and eyes and smiles, like a people forest.

Steven jumps down and sniffs their feet.

'Meet Matias's mum,' Raul says. 'And all his family.'

Raul

Carlos disappears back down the ladder.

Matias's mum hugs me, and his aunt strokes my hair and tells jokes about my moustache and general manhood and makes everyone laugh. His sisters shriek and clap their hands.

I go red and eat the soup and don't translate for Maya. I eyeball her to eat too or Matias's mum will never speak to us again.

We eat and his mum smiles and does impressions of Matias. His serious face. His big frown. His stubborn folded elbows.

Everyone kills themselves laughing and I translate for Maya, who probably doesn't need it – the impressions are that good. The mamis rock on their heels and howl.

Everyone calls older women mamis here. It's kinda friendly and polite. Older guys are papis. It's kinda nice. It makes it feel like everyone's your family.

We finish the soup and everyone gets back to work,

pulling mud out of alpaca wool and weaving it into clothes and cushion covers for the market and the tourists. The floating boats of well-meaning people with money.

Matias's mum moves us over by the window. We sit on the beds made of embroidered cloth and reed, spread across the back of the room. The sunlight starts to fade and the talk and laughter and chink and chirrup of outside drifts into the darkness.

The reeds the beds are stuffed with are sweet and stabby.

One of Matias's sisters points at us and smiles. The others laugh and make noises. Steven tries to put his paw in and out of the spinning wheel.

Matias's mum spreads her skirt and sits down with us.

She smiles at Maya. Maya smiles back.

'Matias likes to be boss, doesn't he?' she says, and I smile and translate and think about how when we were kids he made us bring all the ingredients for potions and remedies he'd created to his house. We all used to line up with our leaves and plants ready for inspection and he'd tick our findings off his list if they were good enough. Or chuck them if they weren't.

'Yeah,' I say. 'He does.'

His mum laughs and speaks again.

'She wants to tell you about the work Carlos does here,' I translate, and Maya nods.

Matias's mum talks fast and stares at Maya like she understands it. Which she doesn't.

'Carlos protects the forest,' she says, and thumps her fist on her heart. 'Many people here hate us, but they have not lived in the trees and the spirits. They don't know what we know. They want *things*.' She rubs her fingers together. 'Money. Food for their children. Clothes. I try to tell them, don't sell your soul so cheap, but they don't listen.

'I don't stop. I don't care. I keep trying. And make my clothes.' She points at everyone working around the hut. The spinning wheel clicks round.

'Carlos works with the police.' She pulls a face. 'It is necessary. And with OSINFOR – *Organismo de Supervisión de los Recursos Forestales y de Fauna Silvestre* – they tell the ships to show their papers, to show where the trees come from. But their papers are false. From non-endangered forest, from lakes even. Carlos has to prove it. If he wins, they have to unload the ships and people lose money. They think if this keeps on,

169

the boats won't come here any more. They'll go somewhere else and people will lose work.' She looks up and lowers her shoulders. 'Carlos risks his life. I don't like to live with it. But I live with what I have to, to keep hope.

'I lost my husband already. It won't be for nothing.' She bangs her hands on her knees.

'Matias stays in the forest,' she says and smiles. 'People say, how can you let your only son live this way? I say, which is more dangerous? Here with you and your threats, not trusting our neighbours? Or with the trees and the spirits. Keeping watch over our home.' She shrugs and raises her arms.

Then she reaches out and touches Maya's hair.

'Carlos tells me you will help.'

For a moment they just sit there staring at each other.

Maya nods.

'This makes me happy,' she says. 'He says you are special, very special.' She stares at Maya. 'He is right.'

Maya goes red and looks at the floor.

'I think you have a secret.' She smiles.

Matias's mum's always been like that. Knowing stuff you don't even know about yourself. Knowing stuff before it even happens.

She stands up, gets a purple flower out of a vase and puts it behind Maya's ear.

'They say the jaguar hides in the shadows but has the most power,' she says, and pulls a reed out of the bed stuffing, puts it into her hand and winks.

Maya holds the reed in front of her knee.

The mamis sit and spin in the corner. The yarn and wheels clicking.

Maya stares at the reed in her hand.

A heron walks across the open doorway and sticks its head round. Long thick neck and bendy legs. It stares.

Maya stares at the reed.

And stares.

And an intense look comes over her face. Calm but focused. And fierce.

I watch.

The hairs go up on the backs of my arms. The mamis stop spinning. The bird squarks and lifts off.

A ball of light bursts out of the reed and gobbles it up like a guinea pig with a daisy, then blows around the house like a balloon leaking air and disappears out the roof.

Maya

I go to wake Raul in the middle of the night. The moon is full.

I tap him on the shoulder. 'Raul.'

He turns over and grunts. He looks funny asleep. 'Raul.'

I poke him and he wakes up. 'We need to get up,' I say.

'Why?' He rubs his eyes.

'Because,' I whisper. I see Steven's asleep in the arms of one of Matias's sisters, his head nuzzled in her chest, as I disappear out the door and climb down the ladder. I sit and wait in the boat at the bottom. The water is quiet. The houses are still. The moon shines out over everything.

I put my fingertips in the water and play with some bright green weed until his face appears above me.

I wave and he comes down.

'I don't think you should be in their boat,' he yawns.

'I want to try it again,' I say. 'I want to call the fire.'

'Now?'

'Yeah.'

'Why?'

'It just feels right,' I say. 'I'm trying to trust what I feel.' I look up at the moon. 'I want to call it in the water. Will you row us into the middle?'

'What's wrong with the house?' He tucks his chin on his elbows.

'It's embarrassing with everyone else around,' I whisper. 'I need to be alone. With you. Like. Us. Alone. It doesn't feel weird with you. It feels like you don't feel it's weird.'

'Compared to Chullachaki and Mapinguari it isn't.'

He does an ogre face and I laugh.

'Rainforest spirits,' he tells me. 'Mapinguari's a one-eyed guardian of the forest who can read people's minds, and Chullachaki is the guardian of the forest who has his feet on backwards.'

'Are they always a "he"?'

'No. There's also a woman with the face of a dog hidden behind her hair, who uses it to eat people's brains.'

'Handy.' I shrug and we laugh together. 'Will you do it?'

'We shouldn't take their boat.'

'We'll bring it back.'

'I dunno.' He rubs his arms. 'Taking people's things is bad. And anyway, you might set it on fire.'

'Don't you want to see it again? Don't you want to see what I can do?'

'Yeah, I do. You're the first magic I've seen for real.' He steps in. 'I like your powers.'

'Me too,' I say. It feels easier to say in the dark. It's what's kept me up, this feeling. 'I want to explore what I can do,' I say.

He nods and the water moves under us as we push away from the house. We row out into the middle of the water. Right out till the glow of the stilt-house lights bob in the distance and the night breeze blows in our face.

And he stops.

And everything begins.

Raul

Maya sits in the middle of the boat and pulls a fresh reed out of her pocket. She holds it up and it glints in the moonlight, like her teeth as she grins.

I think about her dad's wallet in my bag. It feels wrong. Like bad luck. Like I'm calling bad luck to us, like I'm sending out a radar. And Maya doesn't even know.

I take a bag of *chulpe* out of my pocket and pour it into the water.

'What are you doing?'

'Saying thanks to the water spirits for letting us be here.'

'That's good,' she says.

I nod.

'Matias's mum made me understand I need to control it,' she says. 'The reed helps me concentrate.' And she holds the reed in front of her face and stares.

And stares. And stares.

The moon stares down. The wind stops. And bubbles rise up from under the surface.

Maya

The light ball doesn't come out of the reed, it rises up out of the water.

Up it goes. A white light ball like the moon. Strong and bright and floating. Bigger than before.

Then another. And another. Like candle lanterns. They come out of the water and lift into the air like bubbles.

Raul's face lights up.

The balls come together in the sky into one big giant ball.

Raul grins.

And so do I.

The light beams out over the boat. It's so bright I shut my eyes and stretch my arms up. And we sit there and soak it in. It feels like glitter soaking down my arms.

And I hear it say my name – *Maya.*

It whispers.

Maya.

176

And darts all around over the sky, released and flying. Happy like a balloon leaking its air out. Except it isn't leaking, it's growing.

It dives down into the water and we see the ball shimmer right down low. Then it bursts out like a whale and dances round me and Raul. When it goes past, the heat of it warms the goosebumps off my arms.

Maya.

Maya.

'Raul.' I point at Raul and smile.

Raaauuullll,

it says like a howl and stretches out over us. Kind of like a hug. A very hot ghostly fire hug.

And we sit there and grin.

And the night is alive with magic.

Till a boat bangs into us from behind and it goes out like someone switched the light off.

Raul

I didn't notice the boat pull alongside us.

How come I didn't notice? Jungle me would never have missed that.

I rub my eyes. It's hard to see now the light's gone. I reach out, but Maya's already been lifted into the other boat. She tries to fight back, but she's weak and floppy, like all of her power has gone.

I scrabble to my feet, my legs are stiff and my knees won't bend. Their boat pulls away.

I grab the paddle and go after them. Everything is hazy, but I see four dark shapes in theirs. I move towards their sounds. The splashing of the water. Their voices.

They shout something between them I can't hear. The breeze blows in my face. I push the paddle as hard as I can.

There's three of them. And Maya. Their boat sits heavy in the water.

I'm lighter. And fast.

I get closer. The reed boat wobbles in the wake and I nearly lose my balance.

The smell of smoke floats out of one of the houses and a light goes on. A shaft spreads over the water. And I see enough to see Charles and Rosa and someone else.

Someone who holds Maya back as she tries to stand. 'Get off!' she yells and tries to shake him off.

I try to get close. Close enough to jump. Close enough so she can jump back in with me.

Then I hear her say a word that changes everything.

Charles stands and turns and throws something.

I am too limp to react. It hits me in the chin. I fall back into the water.

SPLASH

I go under.

Maya

Two pairs of arms lift me out and drop me into a boat. I can't see, my eyes are dazzled.

'Get off!' I push but my arms are weak.

Two different hands grab me and hold me tight. So close I can hear his heartbeat. I recognise the smell.

'*Dad?*'

'Maya,' he says and rests my head on his knee and strokes my hair. I want to fight, but I can't. It's like all of my energy went out with the light.

I just lie there. I feel weak. And powerless.

And sick.

We paddle to the shore. Someone shouts something. I hear a splash.

'Raul!' I reach out.

'Shh.' Dad strokes my hair. 'He's gone. You're safe now.'

We pull up to the jetty, climb out and get into a pickup.

Raul

The water bubbles over my face and shakes me awake.

'Dad,' Maya said. She's been kidnapped by her own dad.

I swim up and gasp. The boat is floating away. I swim over to it and pull myself out. It tips and nearly capsizes but the hand of the water pushes it back. I'm glad I gave the river the *chulpe*. I wish the waves would tip over the boat in front.

It pulls further away.

I think of her dad's money in my pocket. I wonder if I drew him here?

I see their boat pulling into the quay. And a black shoe bobbing in the water. That's what they hit me with.

A shoe? Were they that desperate?

They aren't tribespeople. They aren't connected to the earth. It figures. The shoe's black with a super-thick sole. You can tell a lot about a person from a shoe.

I squat and look for the paddle and see it drifting out downriver in the other direction.

I look back. They're tying the boat to the jetty.

I can either lose Maya. Or lose the paddle.

Maya stands up and steps out with her dad. If I lose her I'll never find her again.

I lie on my stomach, put my hands in the water and pull the boat along like a surfboard. I have to dip my shoulder down each time on each side to keep me in a straight line. I keep my head down. My eyes down. If they see me again they'll find something else to get me with. Something more than a shoe.

The water carries me. Slick and easy. Fast.

It froths over my hands.

I get closer to the shore.

An engine revs.

I keep tucked under by the jetty and lift my head, so my eyes are just above the wood.

Rosa takes Maya and her dad into a pickup. Maya flops. Charles walks away to another pickup.

I climb out of the boat and reach my fingertips up on to the road for a rock. I ease my catapult out of my pocket. I slip the rock into the elastic and aim for the pickup.

Rosa slams the door and steps on the gas. I watch Maya bounce off down the road.

I keep my aim fixed on the second pickup. Cab for two in the front. Open boot at the back. Charles gets in.

I pull back the elastic. And hold my breath.

My foot slips.

I steady myself.

He starts the engine and pulls away.

I let the rock fly.

SMACK CRACK. Direct hit! The wing mirror shatters all over the ground.

The brakes screech. He stops and I drag my body up on to the jetty and run round the back, fast. I jump over the tow bar into the open boot like a ghost and lie flat, jammed up next to the tailgate.

I lie squeezed against the metal barely breathing, hoping the darkness will cover me like a blanket.

The door slams shut and the engine stops. He gets out.

His footsteps crunch up against the car. His hands curve over the top of the tailgate. Every part of me sweats. If he looks down he'll see me. If he looks up he won't. I can hear his breath whistling out of his nose.

183

'I'll find you, you little rat,' he yells.

I hold myself rigid. But his hands drop and I hear the sound of his voice shout out towards the river, behind the truck.

I try not to breathe and shut my eyes. I grip my knife.

What would I do if he found me? Stab him in the foot and steal the truck?

I've never driven in my life.

His phone rings. 'All right, all right!' he yells into it. I feel him kick the tyre. He slams the driver door and revs the engine. And we go.

Maya

I stand in the hotel room dripping after a shower while all my clothes, Raul's clothes, drip dry (after Dad washed them) in the bathroom.

Raul. I wonder where he is. Wetter than me right now, lost in the lake, alone. I should never have brought him out in the first place.

Being back in this hotel without him feels weird.

I fold my arms and stare at Dad while water trickles down my face and fire burns in my belly, but not in the air, or my fingers – not any more. Dad's presence has put it out like a hose and I fight to let the words come out the way I want before he smothers them too.

'What happened to you?' he reaches for my head.

'What happened to *you*?' I pull back. 'You left me and went to work for JVF? What's wrong with you?'

'I'm so glad you're safe,' he sighs and rubs his elbows like I never said anything.

'I was. I'm not any more,' I mumble into my sleeve.

'You were meant to go home. Why didn't you just go with Rosa? None of this would've happened.'

'How? I didn't even know where you were.'

'Mrs Glidings was waiting.' Dad spreads his fingers like he's strangling the air.

'Why would I go? I wanted to find you. I wanted to know what you're doing. Now I do and I wish I didn't.'

'What do you know about it?'

'Enough. I know you're about to destroy life, ways of life. Generations of life . . .'

'You're taking information from the terrorists?' he yells.

'They're environmentalists,' I say and bury my fists into my elbows.

'It isn't that simple. Trees die. Yes, trees die.' Dad raises a hand and slices the air. 'But with their death comes light. Sunlight. Sunlight reaches the earth and touches people. Improves their thoughts, moods, dreams. One thing is lost, but something else is gained. Something precious. Nature adapts and restores.'

I slap my head on my hand. 'You don't seriously believe that, Dad. You don't. You can't. It's ridiculous. And it's going to ruin people's lives.

'It already has. It already is.

186

'People die 'cos of this stuff. Don't you care? There won't be people left to feel the light. Their way of life's been butchered.'

'I'm not going to cut the trees. The people do that for themselves. They take their own responsibility.'

'They do it for the money. They do it 'cos they're desperate. Or tricked.'

'I don't see many people thanking Carlos Fernandez, do you?'

Carlos. My stomach jumps at his name.

'What do you know about Carlos?'

'I know he took you.'

'He didn't *take* me.' I don't tell him about the fireball and the fact that actually he did. 'Carlos is a good guy.' I look at Dad. 'Don't do anything to Carlos. Everything I did I did myself. Nobody took me. I ran . . . I ran to find you actually.'

I hang my head. All this time searching for Dad. Now I'm here with him and I want to run away again.

I think about Maitas's mum. *People hate us. People give us death threats. We do what we have to do.* 'People would thank Carlos if they knew,' I say. 'They would if there was another way to earn money. If they knew those trees are the lungs of the earth.'

187

Dad shakes his head. 'The burning of the trees enriches the soil.'

'The death of the forest destroys wildlife that won't grow back. Those trees take hundreds of years to grow.'

'You don't understand,' Dad says. 'I'm doing it for us. I'm doing something that'll change both our lives.'

'Like what? What've they promised you?' I think about the letter. The one that promised to change our lives forever. 'Whatever they've promised, we don't need it. We're better off without it.'

He looks at me sharply. 'Don't say that. You don't know that. You don't know what you're talking about.' He goes to stroke my hair. 'Once it's done, you'll see.'

I pull away. 'I don't want it,' I say. 'Whatever it is, I don't want anything to do with it.'

'You will,' he says. He stands up and locks the door. 'You will once you know.' He rubs his forehead and looks out the window. 'I won't take any more chances. I won't let anything else happen, I promise. Tomorrow I'll take you to the airport and put you on the plane home myself.'

Raul

I wake up in the pickup cramped and curled, every part of me stiff. I haven't dared move since Charles left last night.

I look out the back and see the other pickup. Parked up next to us at the hotel. Its smooth white walls reaching up into the blue of the sky. Everyone is in there. Everyone but me.

I look at Rick's watch.

5 a.m.

If I lose Maya I fail Alessa. I fail Matias. And the forest. Everything fails.

I blink my eyes and wonder what I'm afraid of. I know the hotel room, I've been in there before. I know the number. I could just go up there myself, right?

And do what? Run away with her?

To where? Like how?

Charles and Rosa will be there. Guarding her. They'd get me before I even got in. Then who knows what they'd do? If they take me, who will come for me? How will they even know where I am? If they take me everyone loses. Everyone but JVF.

I think about Maya and wish I had magic hands that could reach into the building and pull her out like a fly in syrup.

And a small voice inside me says, *She's with her dad, right? What if she doesn't even want me to? What if that isn't even what she wants?*

Maya

I don't remember going to sleep, but an alarm clock blinks 5 a.m. in my face and tells me that I did.

I shower and slip into Raul's clothes that don't smell of him any more. I wonder how to get out of this. I could run. To where? I've no idea how to get to Carlos's.

I don't know anyone else.

I have no idea where Matias even is.

I look in the mirror and think about Raul. I wish you could reach someone just by thinking. I wish I could teleport. Even if he's in the lake, I'd rather be there than here.

When I come out of the bathroom, Dad's ordered room service and we eat in silence.

The door clicks open and Rosa comes in. My insides shrink.

'Let's go.' Dad puts a hand on my head. 'Things will be different. You'll see. Things will be very different.'

What kind of hold have they got on him?

This is crazy.

He goes to hug me, but I back off, back to the desk. My fingers reach backwards to the briefcase sitting there. The one we found before. The one with the contract.

I click it open, swipe the contract off the top, push Rosa back into the wall and run out the door.

Raul

I climb out of the pickup and look up at the windows at the back of the hotel. I can climb up. Maybe. If Maya sees me she'll know I'm here and find a way out. Right? Even if she's decided to stay with her dad, I need to know. I need to know she's OK.

I look around for handholds up the sheer plaster walls. Breakfast smells drift from the kitchen and my stomach rumbles.

I put a hand out to the wall and kick off my shoes and grip my toes into the window edge on the ground floor. I reach up and don't look down. I pull-slide myself up the wall.

Maya

I run down the stairs lifting my legs up and flying down the banisters with my arms.

I hear Rosa's footsteps behind me.

I jump over the last few steps and out the door into the sunshine.

The light stings. I bring my hand up to my eyes and wish I had sunglasses.

'Oomph!' I feel her body slam into me.

She takes the contract from my hand.

But not before I clock it.

I force my eyes open.

CLICK.

One last snap, I load it into my brain and her arms wrap round me from behind.

Raul

My hands reach for the second floor and I hear a scream round the front.

Maya?

I jump-spring off the wall into a squat and run round the corner, dodging two bikes and a guy with a tray of churros higher than his face. I swipe two and see Maya running out the front.

And Rosa. I'd know her face anywhere.

Her arms wrap round Maya.

'Hey!' the churros guy yells after me.

'Maya!' I run. She's squinting like she can't see me.

'Raul?'

Rosa tightens her grip and walks her over to the pickup Charles has brought round the front and pushes her in the back and slams the door. She gets in the other side. Her dad runs out and gets in the pickup front.

I run over, hammering my hand on the glass. Maya puts her fingers up to the window. Our palms touch either side.

And it drives off.

Maya

I try to open the car door and jump into the street but it's locked. I kick the door and scream. Charles keeps driving.

I hate him.

When the car stops at the airport I try and focus. And squeeze out light balls.

If I did it once. I can do it again. Right?

I grip my fists and try to explode the car.

We stop and Dad opens the door and my inner fire goes.

Rosa pulls my passport out of her bag. They must have taken it from the rucksack at Matias' house. I hate the idea of them going through my stuff. Rosa locks my arm in hers and walks me into the airport where Dad buys a ticket to Glasgow. He shrugs at the price (which is huge) and pays. I think about JVF putting the money in the account.

I want to spit on the ticket. Who wants to fly on blood money? Who wants to fly anyway? Not me.

The flight leaves in one hour. I start to move away from the ticket desk. Dad doesn't. He buys another ticket.

'You're going to Lima?'

Dad hands over his credit card. 'That's none of your business.' He looks away.

'That's a yes then.'

'Something's come up,' he says.

'Like what?'

He takes the ticket and we walk away. 'A meeting,' he says. 'A very special meeting. Something wonderful.' He bites his lip. 'I hope.'

I wish he'd stop talking like this.

'I've been waiting years for this. Years.' He rubs his head. 'I'm not signing till I see something. There's someone I need to see.'

'Then don't go.'

He looks at his ticket. He looks at the flight board. He grabs me in a hug then pulls away. 'Go home. Keep safe. Rosa will look after you,' he says and steps off towards the gate. He looks out at the planes, then back at me. 'I have to,' he says. And goes.

I watch him.

I have to get out of here.

I ball my hands into fists and scream inside till the energy boils up and out. Till a fireball bursts into the air and sets fire to Rosa's bag.

Raul

I kick the earth, and rocks fly up and hit a dented VW. I say sorry to the driver and Pachamama (for kicking her rocks) and put my head in my hands, feeling hollow and hopeless and embarrassed at the connection to Maya that feels like someone just cut.

A car screeches up by my feet. 'Hey!' I put my hands down and jump out of the way and feel lucky I've still got my legs.

A grinning face jumps out of the car. Matias! And a not-grinning one switches the engine off.

'I would have come last night,' Carlos says. 'But someone stole my canoe.'

'I'm so sorry.' I can't look at Carlos. I look at the floor. I feel so ashamed.

I look at Matias. 'How'd you get here?'

'I hitched a lift downriver,' he says. 'To Carlos's. We were meant to meet at Carlos's – what's wrong with you?'

I don't say anything. No way I'm telling Matias about what happened in the lake.

Matias looks round and realises I'm on my own. He stops grinning. 'Where is she?' he yells.

'I don't know,' I say. 'They all went off in jeeps, that's all I know.'

'She went with her dad?'

I nod.

'You didn't stop them?'

'You think I didn't try?'

'Get in,' Carlos says and starts the engine back up. 'We're in Iquitos, the only way in or out is by plane, right.'

We jump in the back and go.

Maya

Rosa chucks the bag on the floor and stamps on it. The fireball floats to the ceiling and I wave at it and run for the exit and out. Slamming into the body of someone running in.

Matias? No way.

'Like how?' I say.

'No time,' he says.

We pull back and grin at each other.

I take his hand and we run to the back of a car, engine running. I crawl in and stick a towel over my head keeping my face away from the CCTV and anyone who might be running out I don't want to see. Matias hits the side of the car and says something I don't understand to someone I can't see.

And someone climbs in next to me and shoves their body against me to stop me falling out and skidding all over the road like roadkill. 'Hey,' the body says.

And I know it's Raul.

My heart jumps and I go pink with relief, even though I'm sweating from lack of air.

I put my hand up (I hope high enough to be his back and not his backside). 'Hey,' I say through the towel.

I think about Rosa realising I've gone. I think about Dad when he finds out. He'll know I'm OK though. Right? He knows I've got friends here now. Well, he would if he'd listened. If he'd listened I wouldn't be doing this. If he'd listened he'd be helping. Not on a plane to Lima.

And I hold my breath while we drive away and don't stop till we've taken three right turns and a left and the air is busy with the sounds of water.

Maya

I burst out of the blanket and jump out the back of the car into the road by the harbour and breathe.

I look at Raul. Our eyes meet.

'Hey,' I say.

'Hey,' he says, and smiles his wonky mouth smile. I think how I thought I might never see him again. The connectedness sparks something in my stomach.

'Did you stop him? Did you try? What did you say?' Matias jumps in front of me.

'How did you get here?'

'He hitched a ride downriver.' Raul winks at me.

'To Carlos's.' Matias throws his arms up. 'We were meant to be meeting at Carlos's. What's wrong with you? Where did you go?'

I think about the night on the lake. No way I'm telling Matias about that. 'Where's Steven?'

'With me.' Carlos taps his chest.

Phew. I think how happy he was with Matias's family.

'Dad's going to Lima.' I look at Matias. 'He said . . .' I think about what he said. That he's doing this for us. I can't say it in front of him. I think about the contract I CLICKed. I need to know what it says. Maybe then I'll understand. 'He said reasons that don't make sense.' I shake my head. 'Scientific reasons. Ones he doesn't believe. I'm sure he doesn't.' I look at Carlos. 'I'm sorry about your canoe.'

Carlos nods and waves his hand.

'If you'd followed the plan everything would be fine.' Matias folds his arms like a kid who can't get everyone to follow the rules. 'None of this would have happened,' he says, and I think how much he sounds like Dad.

'If he wanted you back he'd have come to get you at Carlos's anyway.' Raul shrugs. 'If everyone in Belen knows Carlos, JVF knows Carlos, right? If he was looking for you that's where they'd look.'

I nod. It's true. 'We need to get to Lima. Something's happening. Something big. Something he won't tell me about.'

'I've got this.' Raul unfurls a wet roll of cash from his pocket. 'It isn't enough to fly on. But it's something.' He looks at the ground. 'I took it from your dad. I'm sorry. I think it brought the bad luck to us.'

I shake my head.

'This is for you.' Raul takes a wedge of cash and offers it to Carlos. I think how long it takes his family to earn that from selling fabrics. 'For the canoe.'

Carlos tries to refuse.

'Please,' Raul says and looks at the floor.

Carlos nods and takes the money.

'We could get a boat?' Matias pats the cash and grins.

'Won't we miss him? Isn't that too slow?' I wipe the sweat off my face.

'They're not meeting till Thursday.' Matias scratches his neck. 'That's what I heard. When I was in the lodge.'

'When you were going to kidnap me?'

He shakes his head. 'When Juan Carlos went off with your Dad.'

'Who?' I screw my face up.

'He's the boss of JVF.' Carlos's brow creases. 'Everything goes through him. It's the way all the big corporations work. They have one main guy pulling the strings and running the show.'

'He's just a guy who wants money,' Raul says. 'He grew up in the slums in San Juan de Lurigancho with nothing and wanted more. He's just never stopped wanting it.'

'That's who your papi left you for,' Matias says. 'When he shot at me.'

'He didn't shoot at you.' I hate that Matias keeps saying that.

'He said your dad had to come. He said once he'd seen the evidence, he'd sign the contract.'

'What evidence?'

'I don't know. It sounded like they were meeting someone. Someone hard to get hold of.'

I stare at Matias. 'And you never said that? All this time you never said it?'

'All what time?' Matias pulls a face. 'You made a fire and ran away, remember?'

'OK, OK.' Carlos calms things down with his hands. 'We're wasting time. The boat to Lima takes two days,' he says. 'I need to get us a boat.'

Raul

Carlos speaks for ages on the phone. Pleading, cajoling. 'Yes, they know what they're doing. Yes, they've driven a boat before. Sure, it'll be as good as new, not a scratch, I'll vouch for it.' Haggling over the money. He comes off the phone.

'OK.' He puffs out his cheeks. 'You'll take the boat to Yurimagua, then drive through the desert to Lima. When you get to Lima you go to the office and . . .'

'And?' Matias looks at him.

There is a silence.

Maya sets her eyes. 'I say I'll hand myself in. Say I'll go home with him if he doesn't sign. If he signs he loses me for good. And I'll stay here, with you.'

'Really?'

She swallows.

'It's worth a shot, right?'

'Right.' I try to sound sure. To back her up.

'And I'll make a fire,' she says. 'I'll make a fire so big he can't reach me.'

I don't say anything about how she couldn't before. How she didn't get away last time, how when her dad turned up her light went out.

'OK.' Carlos nods. 'But I can't go with you. They'll want to know where you are. If they think I kidnapped you they'll be back.' I try not to think of all the alliance workers who Matias said have died. 'I can't leave my family,' he says, and we all stare at the floor and don't say anything.

'This way,' he says, and we follow him fast into town to get the keys for the boat.

'Some people want to help,' Carlos says. 'They just don't want to make it public. They want to keep their families safe, so they keep it secret.'

Three guys walk past carrying planks. A path clears through the crowd of people milling about as they walk. In the harbour a boat sits low in the water, heavy with wood. The crew stare at us with hard eyes.

Carlos stares back.

The boat's a taxi ready to take the load out to a bigger ship docked offshore, out of the way, out of sight. That's how it works. There's no inspectors, no papers needed offshore.

'People do crap for money.' Matias spits on the floor. 'It's lives we're talking about here. People's lives.' He goes to yell at the boat, but Carlos stops him. Matias folds his arms and stomps off.

We leave the quay and walk past stalls selling fish and hunks of meat. I see the dark red flesh of a turtle, its head and legs spread out on a table. Maya flinches and so do I.

Carlos hands the cash to a guy at a stall cooking giant white grubs on sticks on a barbecue. He hands over the keys and they nod at each other and we walk on.

Even though it's daylight it's dark and shady here.

We buy water and rice and *chulpe*, maps, torches, towels and rucksacks. I take Aiko's parcel out of my pocket and put it in mine to keep it safe. I buy three wrinkly bags of material from a woman with a wrinkly face who smiles at us.

'What's that?' Maya looks at the bags.

'You'll see!' I say and grin.

It's good to see Maya again. It's good to be back together.

She pokes it and frowns, and we walk back to Carlos, who leads us to the gangway of a rusted river cruiser.

We look at the harbour where the boat filled with wood had been. It must have left while we were at the market. I look at the empty space and think about the empty space that's left in the forest now. The price it paid to load it. Maya catches my eye and nods like she gets it.

Carlos pulls me back. 'Keep an eye on Matias,' he says.

I nod a promise, though it feels weird. Matias has always been the one to look out for us. The look in his eyes says this isn't what he means though. Matias is becoming risky. Since what happened to his dad and Alessa I have sadness. And guilt. Matias has anger with nowhere to go.

The look in his eyes says watch out.

Maya

Carlos says something to Raul that makes him look funny and we stomp up the gangway and on to a double-decker ship that used to be white once but is now mostly rust. We load the stuff on to the boat and clank around. The top deck's bare except for rows of hooks, the bottom has benches and a galley. Below that at the base is the food store and driving seat with a wheel and levers. Metal railings line the sides, and the air flows through the gaps and the holes on the perforated metal floor.

Carlos starts the engine and show us how the controls work. The air fills with diesel fumes. 'Don't sit at the back or you might fall on the propeller and . . .' He slices a finger across his neck.

We nod.

He shows us the levers, which are pretty straightforward actually.

'You got it?' Carlos looks like he doesn't believe us.

Yes, yes, we nod. We get it.

He spreads out a map of the river moving a finger over our journey. It looks so beautiful drawn out. I can't believe we're actually going to sail up the Amazon. He draws arrows on it with a pencil. 'Make the food last,' he says. 'Use the rest of the cash for the bus and for petrol. You take a bus from Yurimaguas to Cerro de Pasco. Then there'll be a car waiting for you.' He taps the cross on the map. 'By then I'll have one ready,' he says. 'I hope.'

Matias gets comfy at the controls and scratches his backside in the seat. He turns the engine over and waves Carlos away.

Carlos pats our shoulders to wish us luck, then backs off down the gangway and waves at us from the shore.

We wind the gangway in and tie it up with ropes and wave back.

I think of his family and feel like the weight of everything pressing on my shoulders is so heavy I might fall straight through the floor.

The boat vibrates and we pull away into the wild cappuccino water and branches scrape along the roof.

Raul

'Wouldn't we be better in the middle?' Maya points to the centre of the river with no trees.

'If you stick to the edges you don't get swept away in the current,' I say and lean over so the wind flaps my hair in my face.

'Right.' She pulls at her hair and we cruise past snakes hanging off branches and trees stooping low into the water. I use the galley to cook meat and rice wrapped in banana leaves. I tie the tops together in parcels and hand them out like Dad taught me. Maya tries to smile but looks so worried her mouth doesn't move much.

The light starts to fade. Me and Maya transform the wrinkly bags of fabric into hammocks that we string across the hooks on the top deck. At dusk I keep my eye out for a small wooden jetty I know is here somewhere and yell at Matias. We stop. The boat doesn't have lights so we can't go on. Matias switches the engine off and the silence shivers round us.

'This is the place, right?' I look at Matias. He nods.

'For what?' Maya looks at me sideways.

'There's a hot springs here.' I smile. 'Where the earth heats the water. It's a special place. Carlos reckons we needed it.'

'He has a point.' She sniffs her armpit and smiles a little too.

I think about the hot steaming water in the worn smooth rocks. I came here with Dad on a fishing trip when the river rose and the water washed us further downstream than we planned. It took a long time to row back up. We stopped off here to bathe. The heat eased out all my muscles. I remember slipping into the hot water like an egg into a pan. I could've stayed there all day.

'Will we get there in time?' Maya frowns.

I think how fast a plane goes. How slow we are. 'We'll go at dawn,' I say. 'We can't continue without light. Go too close to the shore and the boat'll ground – and there's rocks, ones you can't see in the dark. It's dangerous.'

'What if they're coming?' Maya rubs her elbows. 'What if Charles and Rosa are after us?'

I wonder what they'll do if they catch us. I try to push the thoughts away. 'They won't.'

Me and Matias crank down the anchor and tie the boat to two trees to be really secure. We all peer into the dark and get out torches and shine them on to the bank. Two sets of eyes catch the light and run.

Maya points the torch at the water. 'Can't we just bathe here?'

'In the river?'

She nods.

'Not really.' A dragonfly lands on my arm and I brush it off. 'Unless you want to get eaten by an anaconda.' We take out the towels we bought at the market and roll them under our arms.

Matias stares at me. 'We shouldn't all go together,' he says. 'Someone needs to guard the boat.'

'OK. I'll take Maya. You stay here, then we'll swap.'

'What if I go first?' He picks up his towel and squares up to me.

Part of me's sick of being told what to do by Matias. It was easier when it was just me and Maya. 'Ladies first, right?' I say, and realise we've been talking in Spanish and Maya's got no idea what's going on.

'Let's go,' I say in English.

'You all right?' She looks at Matias, at me, at Matias.

'Yeah,' I say, and we clank down the gangway and on to the small jetty someone made who knows when, and up the well-trodden track to the pools.

Maya

I don't know what's up with Raul and Matias. I hear my name though. I wonder if Matias just feels left out that me and Raul get on better. Raul gives off a prickly 'don't ask' vibe, so I don't.

We walk up the path lit by the torches with the jungle buzzing and screeching at us and I'm glad I'm not doing this alone.

'Matias not coming?' I try to sound casual.

Raul looks at the path. 'No.'

I think about the contract I CLICKed. I have to tell someone. I have to tell Raul.

Even though it's night, the temperature doesn't show it. The air's still thick and sticky. Sweat trickles down my legs.

'How far is it?'

'Not far,' he says and slashes back two overhanging branches with his knife that he pulls out of his shorts.

We walk and sweat up the hill to a ridge where the forest opens out and I see the steam before I see the pools. Round hollows with rocks piled round each one to mark them out and steam rising like jacuzzis. The torches mark out stripes of steam in the beams.

They're beautiful.

Raul's shoulders go down and he smiles.

We just stand there for a minute.

'It's beautiful, isn't it?' he says, and I nod.

I feel like I want to hug Raul right now. I want to hug away all the awfulness of seeing Dad. The guilt of running away that I try and push down like a letter under a pillow. The feeling of feeling sick and not knowing what all of this is about. It feels like he'd just get it.

But I can't. I don't.

I'm too freaked out to make that move. What if it messes up everything?

So we just stand there. And I wonder if he guesses I'm tense 'cos he says, 'It's OK, we'll go in separate pools.'

And instead of saying all the things I want to say, and hugging him, I just say, 'Yeah, sure.'

Raul

I hadn't really thought about the awkwardness of me and Maya being here. Together. I just knew she'd love this place. I didn't think it'd feel like *that*. It's kind of embarrassing.

'What do we do now?' Maya says and we hover the torches over the pools and pick out two next to each other.

I check over the pools, fishing a spotted water snake out of Maya's that I don't show her.

'What is it?' she looks over my shoulder.

'Nothing,' I say and chuck it in the trees and hope it slithers far away. 'If we get changed behind the rocks we can stick our clothes on the top away from the ants and just slide in.'

'If we keep the torches pointing up we'll have the light but won't see each other.' Maya looks at the floor.

'Right,' I say.

'Right,' she says.

We change and slip into the pools and the heat

soaks all the dirt and stress of the past few days away.
I hear Maya splashing about in hers. 'Nice?'

'Magic,' she says.

'I know.'

We don't say anything for a bit. And I think about
the lake and Maya's fire and I don't know if she wants
to talk about it or not, but I look at the torch beam
and say, 'What happened to your powers?'

Sometimes talking in the dark is easier. I remember
that when I used to share with my family. It's the time
I'd find Mami or Papi when everyone else was asleep
and they knew I wasn't. I think about how we got
cut off from each other with the walls and the room.
Sometimes things that are meant to make life easier
make it more complicated.

'Dad,' she says. 'They don't seem to happen when
he's around.'

I don't say I noticed.

'Sorry,' I say.

'It's OK,' she says.

But it's not, is it. I try to think of something else to
say. 'You know, in Peru they have a village that has
a rock-throwing festival, where two sides throw rocks
at each other and dodge them.'

'Don't people die?'

'Yes, but it's an honour. Their death's a gift to Pachamama. If someone dies, it brings luck to the village. If no one dies, it's bad luck. When I was a kid I used to want to do it.'

'Really?'

'Yeah, who doesn't want to throw rocks?'

We float in our pools and talk about all kinds of things, whatever comes into our heads. Our breath mingles with the steam and I think about how I've never really talked like that before. How I usually keep most stuff inside. In case it sounds stupid or wrong. I dunno. Anyway it just comes out and it feels good.

And even though the pools keep us apart, it seems kinda close. In a feelings sort of way.

And Maya says, 'Raul?'

And I say, 'Yeah.'

And she says, 'When I was with my dad I saw the contract from JVF. I know what it says.'

'How?'

'I photographed it with my brain,' she says. 'I have a brain like a camera. I photograph things.'

'Like what? Like me?' I grin. She doesn't. 'You never mentioned that.'

'It's kind of embarrassing.'

'It's not embarrassing. It's amazing.'

'Anyway, I think it might be the key to everything.' She pauses. 'It's in Spanish though. I need you to translate it.'

Maya

We dry and dress and walk back to the boat.

I feel a bit dizzy from the heat of the water and slip going down the hill, but catch my balance. It's amazing how good it feels to be clean again. And how churned up my stomach is. I want to know what the contract says, but I don't. It's like a horror film when you want to peek through your fingers and feel sick when you do.

When we get back to the boat Matias is sitting in his hammock checking out stuff on his phone.

'Took your time,' he says and grins at Raul and slaps him with the towel.

I don't know whether to tell Matias. I guess I should. I guess we're a team. I guess we wouldn't be here without him. This affects him too.

'Matias.' I ball my hands up. 'There's something you need to know.' I tell him about the contract and photographing it and how it needs translating. I think he might be angry or laugh at me, but he isn't and he doesn't.

He walks away and unclasps his rucksack and takes out one of his precious notebooks. He rubs a hand on top as he passes it over. 'Write it,' he says and takes a pencil from behind his ear.

'In your book?'

'Write it,' he says again, and swings the towel over his shoulder and heads off up the path.

'See you in a bit,' Raul yells after him.

Matias waves the back of his hand and we watch the beam of his torch drift into the darkness and plink out like a candle.

I look at Raul. And hold my breath.

Raul

Maya closes the book and passes it over. She looks tired and hazy, like she's had to draw deep inside herself to get the words out. Her eyes are slitty.

I read the words and don't look at Maya. I just soak them in and wonder how to make them make sense. It's funny about languages. Knowing two. How words translate into things and meanings and ideas.

How you can know one and be shut out of another. How sometimes there are things that just can't be said in other languages. They don't translate. It's weird.

I think about all these things while my eyes pull the words off the page and my brain tries to make sense of them, changing them into something Maya'll understand.

Words are really a kind of magic code that reveals things or hides them.

'So?' she says.

'So,' I breathe out. 'It says in return for ...'

'Cash?' She flinches.

I nod. 'Your dad will endorse the project.' I run my finger underneath, touching the paper. 'Showing the environmental and biological benefits and significance the availability of light brings. Something like that.' I shake my head. The words are long and hard to translate. My cheeks go pink.

'Go on,' she says. 'It's good.'

'They're offering your dad a deal.' I look at the floor.

'What kind of deal?'

'Your dad signs the contract . . .'

'And approves the project.'

'Yeah.' I nod. 'And they release someone from jail. Someone called Rebecca Fergusson,' I say. She looks away at the name. Her face looks strange. 'Know her?'

Maya

'What?' a voice says from behind.

Matias is back.

We both jump.

'It says he's doing it for—' Raul tries to fill Matias in.

'I heard.' Matias takes the book and traces his fingers over the words.

'Why would he do that?' I push my finger into the floor so hard it makes a little circle on the top. When I wrote the name I knew it though. The gap that's been growing in our house. The thing no one talks about. The name is the piece of the puzzle that makes it all make sense. Suddenly the gap isn't a gap any more. It's a person. Rebecca. The name sticks in my stomach like a sheet of ice. I don't tell them I know it. I don't tell them what it means.

'I guess the only way you're going to find out is by looking it up.' Matias gets out his phone. I try and snatch it away. I know what he's going to find. I don't want to see.

He pulls his arm back. 'What's up with you?' He keys the name in.

I want to run.

I shove my hands under my armpits and let my hair hang over my face.

Matias stares at the phone. He looks at the phone. Looks at me. Looks at the phone like he's playing spot the difference. I guess he's got a photo. I guess the photo shows what I know.

'Just pass the phone, man.' Raul puts his hand out. 'If it was your dad you'd want to know.'

'It *was* my dad,' Matias hisses. 'And it's hers that's destroying everything he stood for.'

No one says anything to that.

Raul snatches it. He looks at the picture.

He turns the screen to show me.

And we look at a woman with the same wonky nose as mine.

With fire hair. Like me.

Raul nearly drops the phone on the floor. Matias catches it. 'Easy,' he says. 'Easy.'

I think I'm going to be sick.

'My mother disappeared when I was three,' I say. 'Maybe now I know where she went.'

Raul

I look at the photo that looks like Maya. But older. At Maya's mum.

Her dad's doing all this to get her mum back?

That's where she disappeared to.

That's where she went?

Maya runs up the stairs and the sky cracks open and rain slams into the roof. It rains so hard it pours off the sides like a curtain separating us from the world outside. From each other.

So hard none of us can talk. If we wanted to. Which we kinda don't.

I go after Maya, but she sits and swings in her hammock like she doesn't want to see anyone. I back off and I sit on the stairs with my head in my hands.

And a thought grows up from my stomach like a bad grub. I try to push it away, but it won't go. Maya's mum. That changes everything, right? I tiptoe down to the galley and unclip my rucksack.

I take out Aiko's parcel and hold it in my hand. I can't let it. I can't.

I stick it back in my pocket to keep it close and make Maya some tea with sugar I find in the galley. Sugar's good for shock. I learned that from Dad. I pass it up and she says 'thanks' and doesn't talk to me, and I don't talk to her either. I have no idea what to say. The news puts a wedge between us like a brick.

How can I ask her to keep doing this?

The rain doesn't stop. It carries on like a waterfall and we hang swaying in our hammocks like three separate islands. In a sea of rain with thoughts that pull us further and further apart. Till we wake up in the night to strange voices and yelling.

Maya

Thud. Thud. Thud. Strange sounds wake me up through the hiss and roar of the rain. Thuds like other boats banging into us. I climb out of the hammock and nudge Raul who's already awake and leaning over the handrail.

The moon is wide and full and lights up the water. And what's floating down it.

Thud. Thud. Thud. The boat takes more bangs to the side.

The water is filled from shore to shore with shapes bobbing and jostling with each other for position, flowing and banging into the boat. It looks like a raft that someone split apart. A wild, loose one, rippling down the river, moving everything out of its way.

It takes a minute to squint through the rain and realise it's logs. The water's full of logs. Dead slabs that used to be trees. Sliced and bouncing downstream. From bank to bank they buck and writhe. At the back, chasing them all down like a herd of cows is a boat. With two figures inside. Poking at the wood with long poles.

'Traffickers?'

Raul nods. 'They cut the wood and wait for the river to rise, then chase it downstream.'

A torchlight cuts across the dark. Lighting the logs, cutting straight across to the herding boat. The guys in the boat squint and block the light with their hands.

It takes a minute to work out the light is coming from our river cruiser. 'Matias!' We run downstairs and find Matias out on deck.

He yells at the guys, something I don't understand. He looks livid and shaking, his eyes wide and hard.

The traffickers pull out guns.

Matias shouts again.

The rain hisses, the logs pound us. I grab his arm. 'Don't!' The torch swings down into the water and cuts across the froth. Raul tries to grab it, but Matias pulls away and yells something. Raul tries to put a hand over his mouth, but he's too late.

I throw myself on the ground. I've never seen a real gun. Never been faced with what bullets can do. I think of the hard metal tip ripping into flesh.

Matias stays standing.

'Get down!' I grab his ankle.

He doesn't. *Crack. Ping.* The gun shoots and hits the side of the boat.

Raul flattens his head on the ground next to mine and I start to shake. 'Can't we hide in the food store?'

Raul's foot kicks me as a shot hits near us and he flinches. Maybe we could make it if we crawled. No way we're standing. 'And leave Matias?'

I stare at him. It's like he has anger in him he can't control. Like it controls him. We need to make it stop.

I look up through my fingers over the edge. Their boat gets closer. Any closer and the dark won't cover us any more. We'll be moonlit targets.

I try to reach into myself and call the fire up. *Ding!* Another shot fires out and Matias yells. They yell back. The rain pounds the boat and the water. I put my hands over my ears and try to concentrate.

But my heart's like a lighter that's run out of gas.

I try to light my lighter.

I flick it and flick it and flick it.

The boat gets closer.

Come on! I yell inside myself. My heart beats so hard it vibrates against the metal of the floor.

BAM. Their boat bangs against the side of ours.

I pull myself up off the deck and stand in front of Matias.

Raul

Maya glows like a ball of fire, a shining ball of light. Lit by the balls that pop out of the air as she closes her eyes and squeezes them. Balls with eyes that burst into the dark like fire bubbles. Hovering round her like angry fire bees.

The rain pours over the edge of the boat. The drops hiss as they fall through the rust in the roof on to the balls. The traffickers boat pulls alongside and they squint in the light. One of them climbs out on to our deck.

One of the fireballs flies away from Maya and pushes him back. The others vibrate with a high-pitched ringing sound. He falls and the fireball pushes, looming over his face like a dog.

'Get back in the boat,' Maya says.

I translate.

He doesn't though – he just lies there and stares at us. Two more fireballs come. They hover over the guy's head, look at each other and dive overboard and set their boat on fire. The guy down there starts yelling and screaming. The guy on deck looks at us, looks at the water, at us, at the water. He gets up and backs off for the boat. But before he jumps he hesitates.

He raises the gun.

'No!' Maya screams.

A burst of fireballs fly from Maya to the gun. To the man's arm, pushing it back. He pulls back, burnt and yelling, and shoots.

BOOM.

Maya stops glowing.

She crumples to the floor.

Maya

Raul crawls over and grabs me. 'It isn't me!' I yell. 'It isn't me!'

Matias is groaning and swearing his head off. He rocks on the deck.

Their boat sails away, glowing with fire and then dark.

The smell of smoke wafts over us.

The fireballs hover over Matias and his leg.

'Get them off, get them off,' he yells.

'They won't hurt you.' I reach out for one. It rubs into my palm like a cat. 'Thank you,' I say. Raul looks at the balls and grins. They wobble-smile back at him. I step over to Matias. 'His leg is shot. We need to raise the wound to stop the blood and get the bullet out.' We step out of the way of the flow that is trickling over the floor.

'Oh my God, oh my God!' Matias keeps yelling.

'Why did you yell at them?' We drag him backwards to the light above the gas stove in the food galley. 'You could be dead. We could all be dead.' I hold his foot up in the air. Blood runs down his leg.

'Those guys just do it for the money.' Matias digs his fingers into his arms. 'They don't even get what they're part of. What they're doing.'

Raul goes to get water, which he pours over the wound. 'We can dig it out with this,' he says and gets his knife out of his shorts.

'We'll need to sterilise it,' I say. I make a fireball hover over to the knife. It bulges like it's squatting and runs itself up and down the blade. 'OK,' I say. 'That works.'

Raul whistles while we wait for the blade to cool and stop glowing. Turning from fire-orange to silver. I think about it piercing his flesh and try not to feel sick.

I squat next to Matias and take his hand and nod at Raul for him to start.

'This will hurt,' he says.

'No kidding.' Matias flinches.

Raul raises the knife.

I beckon a line of balls over to light the wound. I can see the hole refilling like a puddle, blood running and clotting in his hairs. I can't see the bullet.

'Can't we just leave it in?' Matias moans.

'No.' Raul winces and inserts the knife. Matias screams. He pulls out and breathes. 'I can't get it.'

'Go on,' I say. 'Go on.' I grip Matias harder.

He sticks his fingers in the hole the knife has made. Blood squirts out. Matias writhes and screams, but Raul's hands are quick and nimble. He sweats and pulls. Like his fingers are slipping and pinching and grasping at something they can't quite hold.

He pulls them out.

Plink. The bullet drops on the floor.

Raul

I take my shirt off and tear it into strips and wrap it round Matias's calf for a bandage.

Matias wipes the sweat off his face with his hands and looks up. 'You could've backed me up, brother.'

That's all he says. After all that. I feel like punching him. 'That was stupid,' I say. 'You are stupid and you know it.'

If Matias's leg wasn't hurt I think he'd have come for me then. I think we'd proper fight. His face is fierce.

Did I mean it? Maybe it's the shock, or maybe it's something I've wanted to say for a long time.

'Traitor,' he sneers, and I want to rip his face off.

I pull back and hold my knife up. I could slam it into his other leg, but he knows I won't. He's the boss. I'm the little brother, right?

'Cut it out!' Maya yells, and puts her hands between us. Fireballs fly into our faces and push us back.

'Why are you here, Raul?' Matias smiles. 'Did you even tell her? Why don't you tell?' He laughs.

I don't say anything.

'Guys like that killed my dad.' He spits on the floor and stares right at me. 'And his sister. Or maybe he forgot?'

Maya

Raul goes to slap Matias in the face, but Matias grabs his hand. 'Do it, man, do it!' he yells, so close the spit goes on Raul's cheek.

Raul drops his hand, kicks the wall and goes off upstairs.

I put a rucksack under Matias's head and go after him.

The fireballs shrink and follow me. Hovering behind. I turn. 'Thanks,' I nod. It feels like we should spend time getting to know each other. But there isn't time. 'Come on,' I say and coax them in front of me, lighting the stairs. 'We need to find Raul.'

I don't know what to say though.

I didn't even know Raul had a sister.

Had.

I wish he'd said.

I step out on to the top deck. He's sitting in a hammock at the far end. I walk over slowly. The balls bob by my side, glowing in the dark. The boat creaks and we hear the water smoosh and splosh under us as the floor sways.

His back and his folded arms say he doesn't want to talk. The vibe in the air says he has to.

I sit next to him and swing. The balls hover over our heads. Their reflections rippling in the water.

Maybe the silence is like Raul's knife in Matias's leg 'cos after a minute his words fall out. 'This is my sister's necklace,' he says, and takes a white parcel out of his pocket and unwraps it. He pulls his knees into his chest. 'JVF killed her,' he says, 'but it was my fault.'

Raul

The fireballs puff up into transparent lanterns and hover over us, their glow pulsing, warm and soft.

'Alessa. She was called Alessa,' I say. 'She was killed in a tree fall. She shouldn't have been there. She was hiding behind it 'cos I told her to. I was supposed to come and find her, but I didn't. They should've checked the area. But they didn't. It was stupid.'

'Why didn't you go?' Maya says and looks out at the moon.

'I was with Matias,' I say, 'playing football.' And tell her the story, the way I've told it to myself. The way I've run it through my head over and over again.

'That afternoon we were doing one on ones. We drew sticks to see who was paired with who. I got the one no one wanted.

'Matias.

'Matias always wins. Always.

'Alessa kept pulling at my shorts to play with her.

'I sent her into the woods. I said I'd come and find her and told her to hide.

'I watched her run away and thought about beating Matias. That's all I thought about. This time I really wanted to beat him.

'The loggers were cutting close to the village and everyone was trying to act like things were normal, but they weren't. Tension was high. We could hear the saws. Everyone was wondering when they would reach the village. How close they would come. When? But no one was talking about it. Everyone was just getting on with their lives.

'Matias's dad's way was fronting up. He went to watch every day, refusing to leave while they worked. His presence reminding them of what they were destroying.

'Everyone else had football. It was the best escape I knew. The only way to switch everything off. Alessa's way was playing with me. I just wanted her out of the way.

'We kicked off. Me against Matias. I scored first. I dribbled past him and bent it in from the corner. Matias equalised. There was one minute left. I had the ball. I wasn't going to let him win. I wasn't going to let him beat me. I ran at his goal with everything I had. All the other kids were calling my name like a wolf – *Rauulll*. Everyone used to scream it like that. I skidded and fell. I thought I was done for. But I drew my foot back and kicked.

'He wasn't expecting it. He thought I'd gone down.

'It went straight through his legs and scored.

'Everybody screamed and cheered. Nobody beat Matias. Ever.

'I got up. I was so proud. My knee was bleeding, but I didn't care. I had won. I felt magic.

'Then I heard it. The scream. We all did.

'Not cheering. Pure fear.

'I looked up to see people running. "Alessa, where's Alessa?" they were shouting. My mother came, drying her hands on her skirt, running after them. Everything went hazy. And slow.

'The loggers ran.

'When I saw it I was sick.

'Where the logs were piled they had rolled. Squashing two bodies into the earth.

'It wasn't just Alessa under it.

'Matias's dad was there too.'

247

Maya

The words hit me and click everything into place. How Matias and Raul are united by this and pulled apart. How Matias calls the shots and gets to. Raul follows.

Guilty.

He must feel so guilty.

And Matias is angry. So angry it's eating him alive.

'He died trying to save her?' I say.

Raul nods.

'With Matias's father gone, my dad did a ceremony and gave her necklace to the river to set their spirits free. Matias's dad was the shaman. We couldn't shake the bad luck. So we all moved away. To the town. To places with concrete. And cars.

'We kept connected to the water by the channels flowing through our town. The Incas made the channels, pulling water up from the earth to flow down the streets. And the earth magicked up Alessa's necklace. Two years later. Out of the water into our town. Calling me back. It was a sign. It was what brought me here.'

We sit there in the dark. And the moon. Listening to the rain.

'It wasn't your fault. It was theirs,' I say.

'But you want to find your mother, right?' He hangs his head.

'I don't know,' I say and pick my fingers and say the words that have been swirling round my head. 'I don't even know her. I don't know what I want.'

'You might want to see this first,' Matias says from behind and we both turn.

Maya

Matias drags himself along the deck, supporting his bad leg by hanging his arm off the hammock hooks spread out across the low roof, his face lit up by his phone that he holds out.

The fireballs turn to stare at him and wrap around me and Raul. I wonder if we look like two people wrapped in a cloud of fairy lights.

I don't know what it says on the phone but the look on Matias's face tells me I don't want to.

The balls start to lift us off the earth. Away from Matias. They want to get away. They lift us off the boat. Raul grabs my arm. Our feet hover in the air. We go backwards, out over the edge of the boat and then up. Up and up. I see the rust on the ship's roof, the moonlight glowing off the river. Higher, we go higher. We see the tops of the trees. The rain pours on our heads.

'No, no.' I shake my head. 'Down,' I say, 'put us down.' They grumble a low rumble and roll their eyes, but lower us down gently. We land back on the deck.

Matias comes closer, closer. Blood has soaked through his bandages. Thump, thump, thump, his bad leg drags. He comes right up to us and holds the phone out.

I take it.

The page is in Spanish. I have no idea what it says.

I pass it to Raul.

He looks confused and like it touches something inside him that I don't understand. 'It's about your mother. It says she isn't in prison,' he says. 'It says she was an activist.'

I don't know what to say to that. A flash of connection lights in my stomach. We're doing something she would have done? We're doing something she stood for? Then I notice the look on Raul's face. '*Was?*'

Raul hangs his head and looks at his feet. 'It says she died.'

Matias takes the phone back. 'It says she died in an attack on a sawmill,' he says.

'She was part of the EIA?' I look at the floor.

'Kind of.' Matias shakes his head. 'She was part of

the movement before it existed.'

I think of her on the other side of the world. When I had no idea where she was. When I was three and the world snuffed her light out like a candle.

And I had no idea.

I think of me coming back, carrying on the work she stood for without even knowing it.

'The sawmill was dealing in illegal wood. Rainforest wood. Protestors were trying to blow up the machines, but the bomb went off too soon and—'

'OK, OK, stop!' I shut my eyes. I don't want to know.

Matias slides his phone back in his pocket, puts his hands on his hips. 'Guess who owns the mill.'

I look at Raul, but no one says anything. No one has to.

JVF.

Raul

Matias turns and limps away.

'Someone's lying.' Maya folds her arms and yells. 'Someone has to be lying!'

Matias disappears downstairs and starts the engine. Me and Maya run after him. The fireballs float behind her like a long mane of hair.

'You can't drive in this,' I tell him. We look at the darkness sticking to the boat like treacle.

'You want to get there or what?' Matias puts his hands on the wheel. 'I don't want to sleep, do you?'

'You can't drive with that.' I look at his leg. Maya looks like her thoughts are somewhere else.

'I just have to sit down and pull levers.' He shrugs. 'Mainly.'

'Why would my dad believe them?' Maya screws up her face.

'Maybe he has hope,' I say, and don't meet her eyes. I remember the hope I had when they didn't find my sister's body. I hoped she'd run away. I hoped she'd got lost. I hoped she'd hit her head on a tree and forgotten who she was. Now all my hope is out of my hands.

'They probably told him she didn't die.' Matias folds his arms like he's talking about something on TV, something that doesn't even matter. I could punch him. 'They probably said they locked her up and the papers got it wrong. They lie to everyone.'

I kick his good leg. Why's he being such an idiot?

'What?' He raises his arms and the engine's diesel fumes hang around us. 'It's true. Stuff like that happens all the time. People get locked up and disappear. You know it. We all know it.' He looks out at the darkness. 'He was probably desperate.'

'What's *wrong* with you?' I kick the chair this time.

He revs the engine. 'Get out of the way. I can't see.'

'All right, all right!' Maya raises her hands to make us stop. The fireballs turn to look at her, nuzzling up under her arms.

'Let's just get there,' she says. 'Let's go. I'll drive.'

Maya

I separate the fireballs into three groups and send one out front as headlamps. They sit at the front of the boat. Eyes forward. Fire blazing. And two groups for the sides. For sidelights. They stay now. All the time. Not only when I'm angry. Like I can control them better and we're one thing.

I remember Carlos's instructions. I know what to do.

We lift the anchor and untie the ship and set off upriver into the dark. The rain eases to a soft tapping on the roof. Dipping its fingers into the river.

Raul stands on one side of the ship and Matias sits on the other, yelling directions, and if we drift too close to the bank or rocks or someone else's boat. The river rises and the boat flows fast and we swoop like a log out of control. I try to keep it as steady as I can, to keep in control.

Time travels fast on the Amazon in the dark. I lose track of it as Matias crashes into sleep and I watch the moon turn into sky, and the sky turns yellow and blue as the sun comes up. We go past villages built on the shores in clusters. Past women in beautiful colours in boats. A breeze blows over my face. I see a snake dart back into the riverbank, and a boy wearing shorts and eating berries waves. His mouth is red. I wave back. We go by a kid, and his mother pulls him out of the water and looks at us with sad eyes – we shout, 'Sorry!'

I swallow and drive on, rounding a bend, finally pulling into Yurimaguas and the harbour. We bang into the jetty. Just slightly. Just enough that the tyres protecting the front of the boat bounce, and I breathe out.

We hobble on to the shore into the bus station. We prop Matias up on the metal chairs and me and Raul run into town for painkillers and bandages.

We get back panting and Raul makes Matias take the tablets and he pulls a face.

'City pills?' he says.

I think about his dad being the shaman. About the paste he made for my ankle.

'You want to get better or what?' Raul puts them under his nose.

He takes them.

We buy tickets for the bus and cheese and avocado

sandwiches (which we eat like wolves) and chocolate. Thick slabs of chocolate.

I shrink the fireballs down and pop them into an empty peaches can I find in the trash.

'Sorry, guys,' I say. 'It's just for a bit. You can't fly around on the bus.'

They look at me and nod, squeezing up against each other.

We climb on board a big black coach with seats like velvet and I stick the can on the floor under the seat.

I wonder what we look like.

Blood on Matias.

Sweat pouring off me and Raul.

A lady with a big pink shopping bag stares at us.

We collapse into the seats and watch the jungle disappear into rock and desert and sleep all the way to Cerro de Pasco.

The driver yells when it's our stop. We blink awake. I shake Matias's shoulder.

When we get off I pick up the peach can, wrapping it in my shirtsleeves so I don't burn my fingers. I shuffle down the aisle trying to avoid the stares of people looking at my glowing can.

We step on to the pavement and a man sent from

Carlos meets us there, with keys to a car. He looks at Matias's leg while I hide the can behind my back. We thank him and run to the car, dump our bags in the boot.

Matias slides into the front seat, rubbing his eyes behind the steering wheel. Me and Raul pile into the back and I set the fireballs free. They fly around happy and humming. I try to keep them off the seats so they don't burn holes in the leather.

'Keep them away from the wheels or they'll explode the tyres,' Matias says.

I look at Matias's leg, I look at Matias. Blood seeping through the bandage. His face getting paler and paler. 'Do you even know how to drive?'

'I've driven Carlos's car,' Matias says. 'Sometimes. And this is an automatic, so I don't need to use that leg.'

Matias spreads the road map open and passes it to Raul. 'Directions,' he says.

Raul wipes the sweat off his head and I make the fireballs go into the footwell and cross my legs on the seat. They wobble and look up. Matias starts the engine and we swing out into the road and join the stream of lurching and beeping and braking, and head for Lima.

Maya

Raul spends the last of the money on petrol and coffee to keep Matias awake.

Matias hunches over the wheel and we grip our seat belts and try to breathe. Raul's directions are pretty good and we only take a handful of wrong turns.

We drive all day and air turns to yellow dust as we pull away into the desert. As we get closer. Closer to Lima.

I look out the window at buildings growing nearer. Skyscrapers and towers growing out of the desert sand. Matias accelerates round a pickup with three guys bouncing about in the back.

I wind the window down. I feel sick. My insides are all churned up. Everything keeps changing. Every time we find out something new, it's like a jigsaw that keeps making a new shape and now I don't know what to do. I think about Matias's dad, Raul's sister. My mum. Rebecca. Mum?

I think about JVF. Who's lying and how do I find out? If Rebecca's alive, how do I find her? If she's not, how do I prove it? Do I help Raul and Matias? Do I help my dad? I put my head in my hands and I look through my fingers at the fireballs. They look back up at me expectantly. 'What do I do?' I whisper. 'I have no idea what to do.' They look at me and look at each other and start to jiggle. They hum and buzz and rise out of the footwell.

'Whoa!' Raul pulls back and shields the map.

'What's going on?' Matias squints and the car veers.

'I don't know!'

The road turns into a motorway three lanes wide. Cars scream by, the air charges in through the wound-down windows. Horns blow and the air gasps. The fireballs wobble in the wind and merge into one giant bobbly ball.

The fireball spreads out and fills the roof of the car and blocks the windscreen. Like they've sensed something and I don't know what.

'Whoa!' Matias swerves, hits the brakes and screeches into the hard shoulder.

Horns blare. Cars zoom past and rattle us.

The fire spreads and blazes and flickers.

'Can't you keep that thing under control?' Matias flinches.

'No.' I look at the fireball and pull back. I don't think I can. The light shimmers and burns. We sweat. 'What's up?' I look at it.

It squeezes its eyes tight and strains, and two arms pop out of its sides, floppy and weak. It takes a while to get used to them. It's like a kid eating noodles for the first time. They flop around and around by its sides in circles. It seems to enjoy waving them like hula hoops. Then it gets co-ordinated and starts pointing. It points around for fun. Then it looks serious and points out the windscreen.

'Don't touch the glass!' Matias yells.

The fire pulls its pointer back so the glass doesn't shatter.

'You want us to follow you?' I whisper.

It nods.

'We haven't got time for this.' Matias hits the wheel with his palm.

It flows over the back of his seat, raising its arms.

Matias wipes the sweat off his face. 'OK, OK, keep it back,' he says.

And the ball looks pleased with itself. It shrinks a little and hovers between me and Raul and points out the windscreen.

'Straight ahead, Matias – go straight ahead, please,' I say and this time he actually does what someone else says for once. Because I make him. Because the words come up from my heart.

And he hears it.

Raul

The fireball points to the left, we swing off the motorway.

It directs us to smaller roads out of town and on to a dusty track going up into the mountains. Nowhere near the city. I hold the map Carlos gave us, the cross he made on it for the JVF office under my finger. We're well off course.

It points at the floor.

'Stop!' Maya yells, and Matias slams on the brakes and we all jerk forwards.

He puts his hands in the air.

The fire flies out the open window and me and Maya follow. Matias stays in the car.

The fire darts about, looking up down and around, like someone running their fingers over something to make sure it's still there.

It takes it all in. Rubble, bricks, dried-out dirt and bushes. A chicken-wire fence that's melted and warped like something hasn't been here in a long time. A long, long time.

We follow round behind. I have no idea what it's looking for. I just know we haven't got time. 'Maya . . .'

'Come on!' she says, and runs and follows it to a sign.

'This is the place.' Maya touches the rusted holes in the sign that once was white with blue lettering. 'It's brought us here.'

She moves her hand and points to a logo. The sign's old. But we both make out the logo. A globe with a star sticking out the side. JVF.

It's brought us to the sawmill. The one where Rebecca died. Or didn't. It's come to show us what happened. To tell the truth. That's what spirits do, right? That's what Papi Rosales says. Spirits reveal truths. Whether we like it or not.

The fire flies off and scouts about till it finds a clear-ish patch of concrete slab. It hovers near the ground and shrinks and squeezes down to the size of a snooker ball. Compacting into a hot bright ball that glows yellow. Then white. So hot that the ground shines and dry pieces of grass start to burn.

It lowers itself to the ground and the earth burns. And turns black.

The white heat moves.

I hear the car door slam. Matias is limping his way over to us.

'Shh!' Maya puts her hand to her lips and doesn't even look at him.

The fire moves across the earth. Leaving a hot trail. Scorching a black mark. Drawing on the ground.

We watch as it hovers and glows. Barely breathing. Squatting in the sun.

We follow the outline.

It's wobbly and wonky.

But unmistakable.

Maya

The fireball shrinks and floats back into my hands, exhausted.

I trace the scorch line with one hand and the fireball hovers over the other. The drawing's an outline of a body. A body lying on the ground. Me and Raul squat. 'You mean this is my mum, right?' The fire nods. 'She died here.'

It nods again. Exhausted. And sags in my hands.

It doesn't burn. Its heat has gone. It just warms like a stone left in the sun.

'They lied.' Raul hunches next to me.

'I told you, I told you!' Matias says and kicks a rock. Hate radiating out of him. 'JVF always lie.'

Raul takes my hand and squeezes it and we both stand there with holes in our hearts, knowing what loss feels like.

And being there for each other without saying anything at all.

Friendship is a kind of magic. Fragile and lovely.

I hold the fire, limp and small. Losing its glow. Fading.

The dust blows round our ankles. The fire flutters like a chick trying to breathe. Getting colder and colder.

'Don't die on me!' I whisper at it. 'Don't you dare go!' I cup my hands around it and blow like lighting a fire. I hold my face so close my nose is nearly touching it. Tears run down my dusty cheeks. The fire gets colder and colder.

Raul

Maya sticks the fire up her T-shirt and holds it to her heart and rocks on her heels.

'Come on!' she says. 'Don't you dare die! Come on!' She grits her teeth.

'Maya.' I put my hand on her shoulder. She wipes the tears from her face with the back of her hand and stays squatting.

She shuts her eyes and rocks.

She thinks deeply and rocks.

She goes into a trance and rocks.

Maya

I think about roast chicken and surprises and birthdays and laughing so hard snot comes out of your nose.

I think about jumping and cake and cycling so fast it feels like flying.

I think about music and running and trampolines and I feel my heart beating stronger. 'Come on!' I feel my fists clenched and my tears stopping.

I think about sunshine and Socks and peanut butter and chocolate and Raul.

I squeeze my happy thoughts into a tight bundle so hard it's like a glowing ball inside me and I push them out into the fire.

'Come on,' I say. 'Come on! This does not stop here. Come on!'

My belly starts to warm.

My T-shirt starts to heat.

The cotton starts to smoke.

Raul

A hole burns by Maya's heart and the fire flies out woozy and wobbly like it just ran into a building and bounced off.

She holds it between her hands and I want to kiss it, but I don't or I'll burn myself.

Maya stands up. 'At the airport Dad said he needed evidence. He said he was going to meet someone. He said, "I'm not signing till I see something. There's someone I need to see." He means her. He means Rebecca. It's a trap,' she says. 'They tricked him.'

I look at Matias. 'They have a prison in Lima, right?'

Matias looks it up on his phone and nods.

'So if she doesn't exist. She isn't there.' Maya pulls at her hair. 'They're just saying she is. They'll just keep saying it till he signs and then . . .'

'Then he'll find out she isn't.' I look at Maya, at Matias. 'Then what?'

'Then he'll be disposable.' Matias looks at both of us.

We look at each other and run to the car.

'Which way now? Which way now?' Maya says and holds the fire in front of her eyes.

I look down at Rick's watch.

With time we can make plans.

With time we can change the future.

Maya

We drive into Lima. Fast.

The fire is very intense and earnest.

This way.

This way.

This way.

It points.

'This isn't the way!' Matias looks over his shoulder at the map. The car veers.

Raul swipes the map away from Matias and furrows his brow. 'It's true,' he says. 'It isn't.'

'Are you taking us to JVF?' I ask it.

It shakes its head.

'Are you going to Dad?'

It nods.

'I'm not following that again.' Matias swings into the turn-off lane.

'It knew where the mill was, didn't it?' I shout at him. 'It saved your life. You'd be dead if it wasn't for me. If it wasn't for us! You said the forest depends on it. *Everything* depends on it. The forest is full of spirits, isn't it? You believe in those, don't you? What about your dad? He was a shaman. He would have believed. He would have told you to follow.'

Matias doesn't say anything.

But he doesn't follow the map.

He follows the fire.

Raul

We follow the fire to Lima. I've never been before.

It's funny being in the city. Tower blocks grow so high out of the earth and I crick my head to see them. There are tons of cars, three lanes thick, and tennis courts. We drive into a labyrinth of streets. Maya and the fire working as one. Eyes set and serious. It stretches its arms out across the front seat and we stop outside the cathedral.

'In here?' Matias asks it and it nods.

Me and Maya smile at each other and don't look at him.

The fire flies out the window and we follow it into a cobbled courtyard. A blind man is playing music on an instrument with metal strings like a harp with a box for coins at the bottom.

The sound hovers in the air and floats out, snaking between people and under cars and into the rooftops with the birds. When it catches you it makes you shiver and smile at the same time.

He stops playing and beckons us over.

Black vultures squawk at us from the tower and swoop down low over the square towards the fire, their massive wings blocking out the sun. The fire stays strong and does not back off. The birds try to eat it and burn their beaks.

The blind man puts his hand on our arms. 'Shine bright,' he says, and the fire glows and grows. I find some coins and we drop them in his box.

The fire burns too big to hide and we follow it over the cobbles, past people laden down with miniature idols and chains and men with trays of pastries. Everyone gets out of our way. We're like a hot knife through chocolate.

Maya has fire now. Fire she didn't have before.

And the truth.

That changes everything, right?

Sometimes truth's the strongest weapon of all.

A boy walks up the street pulling a huge wooden cart full of sacks of flour with a strap attached to a headband around his head.

He stops and sweats and breathes and keeps going.

So do we.

Maya

When we walk it's like the fire's pulling me. From inside. Like we're one thing.

I can't let it go when I see dad. I can't. I ball my hand into fists and keep it close.

We walk into the cathedral. The air is cool and crisp, and the fire shines and shudders and turns its head, looking, looking.

We follow. Looking too. Over our shoulders, behind our backs. In and out of doorways.

We walk up an old wide wooden staircase and out into a courtyard with shaded walkways round the edges and birdsong like tropical fruit and green plants which reach up like songs to the sun. Thick and green and flowering.

On the walls are painted tiles of men with beards and monsters like dragons bursting out of their stomachs. The bottom halves of the walls are lined with wooden panels that I trail my fingers on.

The fire looks left and right and pulls me.

Bright, alert and growing. As big as a beach ball now.

We go into a room with a painting of Jesus and his disciples sitting round a table eating guinea pig. A guinea-pig last supper. A red devil leans over and whispers in Jesus's ear. I think about JVF whispering in Dad's. I look at a carving of a martyr with its head chopped off. It holds its head with the crossed dead eyes. Me and the fire stare at it for a minute. I think about the sawmill. And sadness flows up into me like a wave.

We hear voices, then see Charles and Rosa are coming down the passageway that links the rooms to the courtyard.

My dad's behind. I want to call out to him, but I don't.

The fire shakes its head and leads us out of the door. Down steps through to cold stone tunnels we have to bend to walk through, lit by flame-torch lanterns that are flickering.

I look either side of the tunnel. There are holes in the floor full of bones. Hip bones and leg bones and skulls look back up at me. Brown without the bodies attached. The church's catacombs.

We stop underneath a grating. Daylight comes

down like a shaft and lights up columns of dust. Music from somewhere else in the cathedral drifts through. Singing like whispers.

Then I hear my dad's voice. I freeze.

We look up through the slats in the grating. He's standing on the floor we're looking up through.

Matias points at the man he's talking to. 'Juan Carlos,' he whispers.

The head of JVF stands in a beige suit. Black hair slicked down. Stubbled chin. His sleeves rolled up and hands imploring my dad.

'You promise proof!' Dad yells. 'You promise a meeting, finally a meeting, and you give nothing!'

'Tomorrow,' Juan Carlos says. 'After, I promise.' He puts a briefcase on a lectern and unlocks it. He takes out the contract and holds it. Offering it out like a gift. 'You sign first, then things are easier. You sign and we have the money. Once we have the money the officials see your point of view. They set your wife free.'

'Tomorrow?' Dad yells. 'Always tomorrow. You give me nothing. I'm a scientist, for God's sake. I need proof. I need facts.'

Juan Carlos throws his arms up. 'We are in the house of God. You cannot lie in the house of God!'

And I realise that's why we're here. Not in an office. Dad doesn't believe them. His heart wants it to be true. His head knows it isn't. JVF can't produce facts so they produce faith. I wonder what happens to people who lie in the house of God. I wonder what spirits do to someone like that.

I think about Raul and Matias's families, their lives split apart. How many others has it happened to and we don't even know? I think about the holes in the forest, opening up like wounds. People and animals cowering from the slaughtered empty space. The spirits angry with nowhere to go.

My insides burn and the fire grows hotter behind my neck. And bigger. I feel the anger and injustice burn up in me till it's white-hot.

I focus my eyes.

And focus.

And focus.

I draw up everything inside myself and scream it out into the fire. The ball bursts through the grating. The metal melts and glows red and bends and clatters on the floor.

I pull myself out of the hole with my elbows and pass a hand to Raul.

He shakes his head and stays hidden.

'Maya!' Dad yells and backs away.

The fire grows. As tall as the ceiling and so bright everyone has to shield their eyes with their arms.

I ball my fists by my side and look at him. He has to hear me. This time he has to hear it.

Rosa and Charles try to charge at us, but the fire makes a ring around me and Dad that no one can get through. We stand in the centre of it.

'It's a trick, Dad,' I say. 'A trap. They're tricking you. You know that, don't you?'

He looks at the light, glowing around us.

'The fire's here because it wants you to listen to me.' I dig my nails into my hands. 'Are you listening?' I look at Dad. At his lost face.

'They don't have Mum. She died,' I say. 'You know that, don't you? In your heart you know it. She died and she isn't coming back.'

The fire turns into white heat, flickery vapour like a mirage, a heat haze.

And a woman steps out.

A woman with my nose and hair and half my face.

A woman like the photo.

Maya

She walks over and lays a hand on our heads.

And we stand there.

Holding each other and not saying anything.

She puts her arms round both of us and we hold her tight back. Our backs glow in the circle, time stops, the world melts away and nothing else seems to exist.

I don't know how long we stay like that.

I just know I don't want it to end.

She looks at Dad and they raise their fingertips to each other. 'Your daughter is your light, Handi,' she says. 'How could you be so blind?' Dad looks at her. Tears fall down his face. 'Just because I was gone you could only see darkness.' She sighs. 'Stop searching the world when what you're looking for is here on your doorstep. What you need is love. Catch it before she grows up and goes.'

Dad hangs his head.

She pulls back to look at me. There's so much I want to say, but nothing comes out. She strokes my hair like she knows it. 'Nice spirit, Maya.' She smiles. 'Strong and proud and true.' She puts a hand under my chin and lifts it up. 'I'm so proud of you.' We look at each other with an intensity that I try to soak up and hold on to. The heat starts to cool.

She starts to fade.

She points to the hole in my T-shirt. 'I live in here now,' she says. 'Don't let me go out.'

'Don't go.' I bite my lip and hold her tight.

'It is time.' She closes her eyes. 'This is the end of it,' she says.

Hot to warm, to cool, to a soft breeze.

The fire dies.

And we stand there, Dad and me holding each other.

Raul

I look up at Maya and her dad through the gap in the floor. I look at the metal grating warped and fading from red to black. I look at Juan Carlos as he walks over and puts a hand on Maya's father's shoulder.

'Leave us!' her dad roars. 'Leave us!'

Juan Carlos steps back. He takes out a lighter and flicks it and burns the contract on the lectern. I don't know if he's burning the evidence or if it's a sign that the deal between them is broken. 'Very well,' he says. In a way that sounds like it hasn't ended. That he hasn't finished with Maya's dad at all.

A flaming piece of ash falls on to the floor. The wind blows down through the tunnels. Up from the bones. An invisible puff of air flutters the paper on to the man's trousers, back into life.

They catch immediately.

Juan Carlos shakes his leg and smoke drifts up to his waist. I watch with horror as fire starts up his leg, getting higher and higher, crawling across his chest and over his body. Charles and Rosa shrink back up against the wall, Maya and her dad are turned away with no idea. He screams. I feel sick, but I can't look away.

A thought sparks in my head and I stop it. Without him, what would happen? Would JVF even exist? The flames rise. Covering his trousers, his arms, his face. It'd be fair, wouldn't it? A life for so many lives. My stomach says to let him burn. My heart says I can't.

I jump out of the grating.

Matias grabs me. 'Leave him!' he yells.

I shake him off. 'Water,' I scream. 'We need water!' There is none.

I take my shirt off and start hitting the flames. But each flap fans them. Smoke alarms go off and guards come running. Yelling. I run to the wall and rip an extinguisher off it. Matias follows dragging his bad leg behind him but it sticks in the grating. He falls to the floor. And doesn't get back up.

I pull the plug out of the extinguisher and spray. The foam puts out the flames. Juan Carlos drops to the floor. 'Matias!' I yell but his eyes are shut and he says nothing. The cathedral guards run in. What if they catch me. What if they think I did it? I pull Matias up off the floor. His arms over my shoulder and lift, limping along to the grating and jump down, crumpling under his weight.

Raul

Maya and her dad jump down through the grating. Maya's dad lifts Matias off me and hauls him over his big broad shoulders. Maya offers a hand and pulls me up and we run. No time to talk. Clattering down the labyrinth of tunnels past the bones towards the light.

We run and time seems to slow. I think of all the spirits in here. How spirits pass between this world and theirs through stone. How you can call them up with objects. Something precious to them. How Papi Rosales used to say that when babies cry you take them to the cave to call back their spirit guardian to make them stop.

We reach the end of the tunnel. The sun shines off a small yellow window.

Maya and her dad run out.

I freeze.

The shadow of a small body squats behind the window waving at me, beckoning. I wonder how long till the guards are here. I hesitate. I see two pigtails and shiver. I go towards it. I have to.

Two hands press up from the other side. A nose presses up against the glass. A face I know. I feel the necklace pressing up against my leg in my pocket as I lean into the wall.

'Alessa?'

She pushes her nose on to the glass so her face is squashed. I press my forehead up against it too. Put my hands up so our palms touch either side. We stay like that. Touching and not. Close and apart.

'I'm so sorry,' I say. I know it's simple. Too simple. But somehow there's power in the words.

I am sorry.

The shadow of guilt sits on my back. Heavy and listening. I can't set it free on my own.

'Love you, Alessa,' I say. Pressing my fingers into the glass. My breath steaming it up.

I wish I'd said it more.

'Love you, big brother,' she whispers. 'Not your fault,' she says, and shakes her head and giggles. Like she always did.

Alessa was like rainbows. She had joy that turned up when you weren't expecting it.

The guilt shadow clings on and won't let go. *You can't forgive yourself for what you've done. Only the people you've wronged can do it.* Maybe that's not true though. Maybe that's just thoughts not facts.

And I need to let it go.

'Love you, Alessa,' I say.

'Not your fault big brother,' she says and draws a smiley face in the window steam.

I smile as the tears flow. And let her words sink in. They're like light. The shadow loses its grip. Like a flame on a leech. 'Not your fault,' she says and shakes her head and it falls away. And scuttles into the dark. I feel lighter. Like I can breathe. I wipe my tears with the back of my hand and grin back at her.

I draw a smiley face on my side and she smiles.

And our hands touch either side.

I hear footsteps down the tunnel.

I have to run.

I can't.

I can't leave her again.

'Raul!' Maya turns and yells.

Maya

We run to the car and Dad props Matias into the passenger seat. I root round in his pockets for the keys, chuck them to Dad and look around for Raul. Raul?

I run back through the courtyard and grab him. I don't know what's got into him, but he looks totally freaked out. And he's crying.

'Come on!' I grab his hand and pull him along, away from the yelling and the footsteps coming from the other end.

We run. We run like firecrackers are tied to our butts, through the courtyard, past the music man who plays and grins, and into the car. Dad's started the engine. We slide into the back. Matias sits slumped in the front.

'Is he OK?' Raul looks at Matias.

Matias squirms and groans.

'He's breathing. He'll be OK,' Dad says and looks in the rearview mirror.

A fire engine screeches up. Blocking the road. An ambulance pulls alongside it.

Dad pulls his hair. 'Where to? Where do we go?'

'Just go.' I look out the back windscreen at the guards with batons and guns swarming out.

Dad reverses down the street.

Raul grips Alessa's necklace in his hand. 'Go to the sea,' he says.

And we go.

Raul

We drive through town. Looking out the back window, listening for sirens.

Cars pile in the road from all over, honking and music pounding out the windows. Sirens come and go, but none are on our tail.

We pull over by a park on the cliff and jump out of the car. Maya's dad carries Matias and we push through the swarms of tourists milling round the giant statues and sitting on the mosaic walls drinking cool purple *chicha morada*.

We carry Matias down the cliff steps to the sea. Just the sound of it makes my skin prickle. I want to take Alessa back to the water. I want to set her free.

I've never seen the sea. It takes my breath away.

The salt dances on my tongue and catches in my throat.

The water pulls and pushes the shingle rocks in and out and the voices from the crowds above drift away soaring with the gulls.

We prop Matias's head up on a rock and I bring water in my cupped hands from the sea to pour over his face.

'Matias?' I blow air into the water and rub his forehead.

He sits up and rubs his face.

'I'm sorry, I'm so sorry.' Maya's dad squats next to us and cries, like the enormity of everything hits him and the pain needs to come out.

We all just sit, staying like that for a bit.

'You didn't sign the contract though.' Maya puts a hand on his back. 'You didn't.'

He shakes his head, pulling himself up and offering a hand.

'Matias,' Matias says and takes it.

'Raul,' I say, and he shakes both our hands.

'Maya,' Maya says. 'Remember me?'

He throws his arms round her and they sit there and hug and the sound of the water pulls the pain out of all of us for a while.

Maya

Me and Dad go to the edge of the sea to be alone and talk for a while.

'Why'd you never tell me about her?' I shove my hands under my armpits.

Dad sighs. 'You were only three.'

'So?'

'So. I loved her and thought she'd come back.' He puts an arm round my shoulders. 'I couldn't stop her coming here. I couldn't keep her safe. So I didn't really tell anyone. Then it got too big to tell.'

'You can't stop everything from happening, Dad.'

I think about him trying to keep me safe. About our rows.

'I know,' he says, and shakes his head. 'I know.'

'You should've said.'

'They never showed me the body and I never believed them,' he says. 'I couldn't tell you 'cos I didn't know. I couldn't tell you something I didn't believe.'

'You could've just told me the truth.'

'When they didn't find the body, I thought ...'
Dad hangs his head. 'I thought maybe she hadn't
died. Maybe she just left us. All I could see was
darkness. So I put everything into my work. Looking
for light. Looking for something to believe in again.'

'Then JVF sent you a letter, right?'

'They came to a lecture I did on climate change. It
was contentious. I was arguing that the world adapts
and restores. It was meant to be provocative. They
took it literally.' He rubs his face. 'It was stupid. They
met me afterwards and offered me money to endorse
their project. A collaboration. I wasn't interested.
When I refused they sent the letter.'

'Saying they could help you find her.'

He nods.

'When you want something so badly your heart
takes any hope anyone gives. You were growing up
and started looking and acting so much like her it
was too hard to bear. You needed her. I needed her.'

'I need you too, Dad. But you shut yourself away.
You don't talk to me. Or listen.'

'I know,' he says. 'I know. I'm so sorry.'

We stand there for a minute and I put a hand on
his shoulder.

'You're so much like her,' he says.

'I guess.' I think of her spirit. 'But I'm also me. I think you need to get to know me again,' I say. 'I think you've got some catching up to do.'

Dad ruffles my hair and breathes in a big long breath. 'True that,' he says and wipes his nose on the back of his hand. 'So what do we do now?'

I look at the sea and the sky, the paragliders taking the risk to jump off the cliff and float down. 'You switch sides. You do what Mum did and work with the alliance. You back up Carlos.'

Raul

We sit on the beach watching the water going on forever.

'I just want everything to go back to how it was, you know,' Matias says. 'I want our old life back. Don't you?'

'Even if we went back it wouldn't be the same.' I hang my head. We take turns throwing pebbles. Seeing who can get them furthest. I hold one up. 'It wasn't our fault, about your dad, about Alessa,' I say. 'It wasn't our fault.'

'It was mine,' he says and throws one right out to sea. 'I know it. It was mine.'

'I never knew you thought it was yours?' This revelation jolts me. I drop all the stones through my fingers, watching them fall. 'It was JVF's,' I say, 'not ours. We couldn't stop it. It's just how it was.'

I can't get over that he thought it was his fault too. All this time. All this time I've been carrying it on my own.

If only he'd said.

If only we'd talked about it.

But the words stayed deep in us. Too deep and raw to take out.

'I think we just have to let it go,' I say and take Alessa's necklace out and hold it up. 'You got a minute?'

I stick my finger under his armpit till he smiles.

'Sure,' he says.

I get up and dust the sand off my butt and take his hand and pull him up off the floor and we hobble to the water's edge.

We stand there listening to the ocean waves and I take Alessa's necklace and throw it out into the sea, back to the water.

We let it go.

Arms round each other's shoulders.

I wonder if it'll come and find us. If it needs us again.

Then I do something I've needed to do for a long time.

I borrow Matias's phone and ring home.

Home.

I guess it is now.

I guess I have to get used to it.

Home's more about people than places. Right?

I click the buttons. And hold my breath.

'Papi, it's me,' I say and hold the phone away from my ear while he fills it with relief.

Maya

Dad puts us all up in a hotel and me and Matias and Raul spend the night taking baths and hitting each other with pillows on giant beds and watching bad TV (while Dad spends it on the phone to Carlos). Then feasting on charcoal roast chicken so crisp the skin crunches and juice runs down our chins, with fries and garlic dip and Coke that froths in our bellies.

Matias gets stitches in his leg from the hotel doctor and me and Raul stand on the balcony so we don't have to watch.

We listen to the faraway hiss of the sea and the yelling of the kids playing football down below as the street lights come on.

I take his hand. There's a flicker between us and we stare straight ahead not looking at each other. Kind of knowing that this is the end. And kinda of not wanting to say it.

'So that's the end of it,' I say.

'I don't know,' he says. 'I reckon if Alessa's necklace can travel thousands of miles up the Amazon, you could always catch a plane.'

And the balcony fills with fireballs which hum gently, hovering up against each other.

'Where do you think they come from?'

I shrug and tell him something Dad told me years ago. 'You know we're all made from the same materials as the sun,' I say. 'There's a bit of sun in all of us.'

And Matias pushes his face against the glass and makes faces through the window.

Raul

We stand at the airport and Omar comes over and we do our special handshake and he slaps backs and shakes hands with Matias and hands me a box of travel-sickness pills.

'Thanks,' I smile and take two.

'I'll come back for you tomorrow,' he says to Matias, and gets into the cockpit.

'You sure you don't want to come back and stay with us?' I say.

Matias shakes his head and shows me the environmental projects we looked up last night on his phone. Where people come from all over the world to help. 'I was thinking of starting one of these,' he mumbles. 'Maybe. Maybe we can set up a project in the old village.' He smiles

'Nice.' I raise an eyebrow. 'Just try and be a bit less bossy, OK.'

He elbows me in the ribs.

'You might want to try talking to them,' I say and

shuffle my feet. 'Sometimes it's hard to know what you're thinking.'

'Trees don't do much talking,' he says and looks at the floor. I guess trees are all he's had for the past two years. Pretty much. I'm glad that's going to change.

I put my arms round his chest and hold him. He holds me back.

No way either of us is going to say 'I love you, man' but that's how it feels.

Sometimes feelings are stronger than words.

Omar starts the engine and we jump.

'Come back and see me, townie,' he says. 'So jungle you doesn't get extinct.'

And we wipe our eyes and pull away.

Maya

I shuffle past Dad into my seat and watch the brown snake of the Amazon winding away out the window. I think of Raul down there. Us pulling away from each other. And it hurts. A bit.

I look at Dad. And take a breath. 'I've got a list of changes I'd like to make when we get home,' I say.

'Right,' he says, and looks at me sideways and winces.

And I start on the list I've been making since Raul left this morning. Dad writes it down.

And he winces again. But he listens. Because this time I make him.

And it's not like we can solve everything just like that.

I know it.

Changes happen in pieces. Small chunks at a time.

You can't fix it all. But it's a beginning.

And beginnings feel good.

Raul

This time when we fly I feel like a bird. Free. I trace the rivers out the window with my finger and watch the landscape turn from desert dust to mountain.

I think about Maya on her plane.

Us floating apart. It feels kinda weird.

We bounce on to the ground and I am not sick.

I give Omar the thumbs up. 'Nice work, Tigger,' I say and take the headphones off as the plane rolls and then stops.

An old bumped Toyota meets us at the airport. Diane gets out. 'Papi Rosales is my grandpapi,' she says and holds up her phone. How come I didn't know that? 'He said you guys needed a lift.'

And I grin and think how fate plays games with linking us all together.

The universe is bigger than we know.

We hug and me and Omar get into her car and I sit in the front while Omar naps across the back.

When we see Dad he runs and hugs us both. And

Mami piles in and my little brothers hug my legs. I am like a hug tree.

Omar and Papi look at each other with grins on their faces and wet eyes and arms round each other's shoulders.

'It's been too long,' Papi says and pats Omar's shoulder.

'I know,' Omar says and does the chicken dance and makes us laugh till snot squirts out my brother's nose.

Papi cooks *aji de gallina* (creamy chicken curry) and chocolate bananas 'cos he knows I love them, and Mami strokes my hair and kisses the top of my forehead. I help wash up.

'Alessa visited me,' I say and I look out the corner of my eye and stack a plate. 'She looked happy,' I say. 'She says she forgives me. She says everything's OK.'

'It always was,' she says. Tears roll down Mami's face, but she puts down the cloth and smiles and holds me tight. 'It wasn't your fault. I never thought that. You know it, right?'

And we stay there like that till Papi Rosales's dog comes in and rubs his nose on my legs and wags his tail and barks.

'Toffee!' I say and hold my hands up, and he jumps and puts both of his paws on my chest and licks me in the face.

He goes back outside and leads me to Papi Rosales.

Papi leans against his wooden door and flicks grit at the wall. 'It's time,' he says.

'For what?'

'Your story,' he says and closes his eyes. 'This time it's your turn.' He grins and pokes me in the leg with a stick.

I smile and ruffle Toffee's ears.

Maya

I sit on my bed with Socks and type out a message to Raul.

I now have a camera so I send him a picture of Dad's face when he comes in the door with a carry out.

It's bright. And kinda proud.

And happy.

The kind of look that comes and goes in a bazillionth of a second.

Like the one he had yesterday when he came home with an iPhone and I gave him a thumbs up.

CLICK.

I take one for my brain.

And one for my phone.

And take one of what he looks like right now while we're laughing at Socks who's bopping the fireballs that got so excited they flew out of the lampshade.

Raul

The water runs down the streets.
   Same as it has since the Incas.
   Time flows on.
   I look down at Rick's watch.
   With time you can escape to put things right.
   Then you don't need to escape.
   Not any more.

And my phone buzzes in my pocket . . .

Author's Note

Thanks to the support of the Arts Council I spent three weeks travelling throughout Peru with guide Gaspar and an intrepid group of travellers. From the city streets of Lima, to canyons and islands and volcanic towns, floating in lakes, climbing up enormous mountains and into the Sacred Valley, the heartland of the Incas, meeting genuine people and soaking up customs and beliefs and atmosphere that became Maya and Raul's adventure (and Raul's home town!).

The trees and creatures in the book are all real. As, unfortunately, is illegal logging. It's a big problem in Peru and people literally risk their lives standing up for indigenous people and the forest. Thankfully the EIA and OSINFOR also exist, though all the characters in this book are fictional.

The Rainforest Alliance and Rainforest Foundation also run wonderful conservation projects. You can find out more about them and what we can do at www.rainforest-alliance.org and www. rainforestfoundationuk.org

Acknowledgements

This book has been a very intense ride of a write and wouldn't have happened at all without the incredible kindness, friendship, support, wisdom and love from so many people. Your support makes me see the magic in the world! Thanks for being there.

To Chris, Tom and Wilf. Thanks for all your patient insightful and invaluable listening! Thank you, Tom, for your sharp ear and honest take-no-BS attitude. Thank you, Wilf, for your laughter and kind, shrewd observations.

To (our cats) Iorek and Bob who joined me every writing day with furry huggy encouragement.

To Tom and Ruth and Guy and Bea, who lent me their cottage out of pure kindness, so I had somewhere to warm and cosy to go and didn't have to scrape the ice off my caravan windows – THANK YOU! You're very inspiring, wonderful people.

To my friends, ALL of you, and in particular (in alphabetical order): Katie and Charlie and Edy Darby-Villis, Liz Flanagan, Rachel Harker, Penny

Lee, Pamela Matthews, Theresa Webster and the Hexham writing gang – who were always there with wisdom and a laugh when I needed you. You're amazing. I am so lucky you are in the world.

To the brilliant Faber team – in particular the steady and sage Natasha Brown and my editor Stella Paskins, who just plain got what I was trying to do. Honest, supportive and wonderful. Thank you.

Thanks to my wonderful agent Catherine Clarke and her savvy, safe hands.

To David Almond for being such an inspiration and support in his work and in himself.

To *Yoga with Adriene* – hand on heart this book would NOT exist without your YouTube channel. Yoga for everything in any moment you need it, for FREE – constant and transformative support. It's been a revelation at the start and end of every day.

To all the amazing fellow authors out there – it's so good to meet you and be part of the big author family.

To my *family* family, right behind me on this writerly rollercoaster: Thanks, Dad, for sage advice and the hairy eyebrow fact! Thanks, Mum, for the kindly ear and support. Thanks, Em, for being there and making me laugh from all over the world!

To the wonderful Arts Council who supported me in the writing and research of this books, and the brilliant Cragside and Eastlea schools in Cramlington who went on this journey with me in spirit – setting travel quests and sharing in all of the discoveries with brilliant insights and enthusiasms, big-hearted emails and Inca Cola tastings! Much appreciated. Keep up the wonderful writing and reading! Here's to the fantastic Mrs Bilton and Mrs Stafford who are inspirational people and teachers and make the world brighter place.

To my Peru companions – especially Jane! (And obvs Gaspar!)

To Juan Carlos Galeano and his book *Folktales of the Amazon*. I learnt so much from this and you. Thanks so much for collecting and sharing it. It's a brilliant book.

And thanks to YOU, the reader. Without readers what's the point of books? You make the words come alive. Thank you!

LOTTERY FUNDED | Supported using public funding by
ARTS COUNCIL ENGLAND